# BETTER LATE THAN NEVER

## ADA AUSTEN

Disclaimer:
This is a work of fiction. Names, characters, places, and incidents are either the products of the author's imagination or are used fictitiously. Any resemblance to actual persons, living or dead, businesses, companies, events or locales is entirely coincidental.

ASIN: B08J7KF5MJ
Paperback 5x8 ISBN: 978-1-7358198-0-8
First Edition

*ACKNOWLEGEMENTS*

Thank you to NANOWRIMO for enabling the first draft of this novel in November 2016.

Thank you to Steph and Jesse for reading it and giving me invaluable feedback.

Thank you to Lisa for being my writing buddy and giving chapter by chapter feedback on revisions as I wrote them.

Thank you to the betareaders, especially Latoya, Star and Grace, for honest, yet supportive feedback.

Thank you to Byron for your kindness.

Thank you to Dalton for your openness and for choosing to find the good.

Thank you to Romance Twitter, Writing Twitter and Native Twitter for all the lessons you take the time and energy to share.

Thank you to Kirby, for always waiting for me no matter how slowly I walked on our daily beach walks out on Sandy Hook, while I gathered the gifts of the sea and discovered the story of Carrie and Manny.

Thank you to my husband for being brave enough to marry this Jersey Girl.

Thank you to my family. It is your love that allows me to write this book of love.

Thank you to the Lenape, the original caretakers of the land and sea where I live.

Thank you to the Chiricahua and Mescalero Apache for inspiring a humble, compassionate and generous hero.

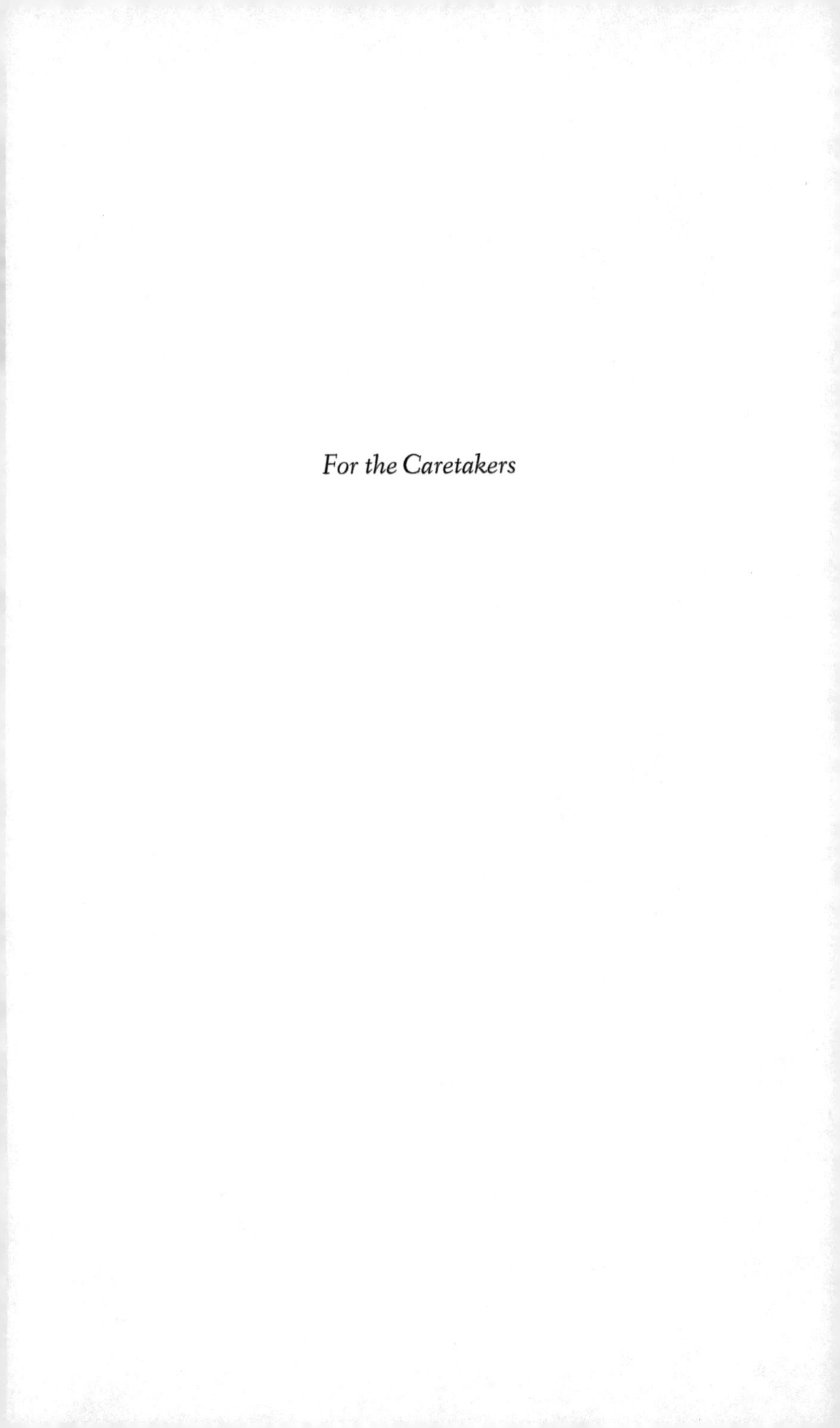

*For the Caretakers*

The room was the exact opposite of the space he needed.

Manny leaned slightly to his right and let his leather backpack slide off his back onto a nearby seat. The strap of the bag tugged his long hair as the bag fell. Why hadn't he tied the hair back this morning? He pulled an elastic off his wrist and smoothed his hair into it.

The room was a large lecture hall, set like an amphitheater. He walked around it slowly, checking the viewpoints from various seats. Every seat was placed so a student could clearly see the podium. And nothing and no one else. How did they expect anyone to learn here?

Maybe this new job wasn't going to work out for him. He hadn't even considered that.

A student entered. "Architectural History 101? Professor? Professor Chadda Chat Ski?"

Manny laughed, moving back towards the door to shake the outreached hand of a tan dude with spikey blonde hair. "Manny Chattoche," he said. "Students usually call me Professor Man. That's easier for some reason."

"Cool. Professor Man. I'm Rick. Hey, I think I've seen you early mornings this week, out on Seven Presidents beach?"

Manny nodded. "Early, yes. I don't remember seeing you, though."

Rick laughed. "That's because I'm suited up. I'm the one catching the waves."

"That explains it. Running is more my style."

"And working out?" said Rick, eyeing Manny's biceps.

Manny looked down at his arms. He had become obsessed with seeing how much weight he could lift and how finely he could tune his body the past six months. His brother Cochi teased him about it that it was to impress Carrie when she saw him again. Manny hadn't thought about the reason. He had just felt driven to do it, so he did it. But Cochi was probably right. His teasing was always right on target. Why hadn't he worn long sleeves today?

"I'm not sure I'll be able to continue with the weights," he said. He hadn't come to New Jersey to spend weekends in a gym, at least he hoped he hadn't. Unless, of course, Carrie went to a gym now.

He moved towards his backpack. He needed to stop thinking about Carrie.

He checked the registration list for Rick's name. There were only ten students in the class. Why had they given him such a big hall for such a small class? Why did he think it was going to be different here? There was always some type of friction itching him.

"Students for Architectural History 101, you can all sit in the first row," said Manny to Rick and the other students that were gathering at the door. "I'll sit on the edge of the stage facing you. That's the closest we'll get to a circle."

"It's an interactive class, not a lecture," he explained as

they sat down. "In my classes, every one of us, you and me, have something to share and learn. To start the class, we introduce ourselves in what I know as the proper way. Tell us the name of the people you come from and your name, the place that you come from and where you live now. If you'd rather not, that's okay too, just tell us how much is comfortable for you.

"I'll go first. I was born and raised on the Mescalero Apache Reservation in Mescalero, New Mexico. I went to Rutgers University here in New Jersey for my undergrad. Then I went to California for my Masters and Doctorate. I was teaching there until a few months ago. Now I live here in Long Branch, New Jersey, just a block from the ocean. The people I come from are known as the Chiricahua Apache. My name is Mangus Chattoche. Most people call me Manny or Professor Man."

The students followed his example. He was surprised that more than half of them weren't from New Jersey.

"Next, in our classes, we recognize where we are," said Manny. "This originally is the land of the Lenape, a peaceful people, known as the grandfathers because of their wisdom. We acknowledge them. We're grateful to be in a place where thoughtful learning is valued. The mansions here on this campus were once the summer home of a U.S. President, Woodrow Wilson. We'll be touring some of the buildings, examining their styles and recognizing how they influence this school."

Manny stood up and picked up a handout he had prepared.

"Before I forget, let's talk about your first assignment. This week you'll write an essay titled 'Home'. Try to answer these questions in your essay. What defines a home for you, personally? Where is home? Must it be in a certain country or state? Must it be near an ocean or a certain mountain? Is it the pillow on the couch, the photographs on the wall that define home to you? The angle of a certain constellation in the night sky? Is it made of a certain material in a specific structural style?

"Also, please detail what you need in the place that you live. For example, a desk, a bookshelf, a workbench, a big kitchen? If you live with others, list their needs too."

"Are we defining our dream house?" asked a female student.

"Keep this limited to a space that has everything you need for yourself and those you live with, but not more than that. Dream houses tend to be excessive, not rooted in our true needs or lifestyles."

He saw a few frowns. These kids weren't getting it at all. They were bored already.

"You might think all this doesn't matter, to be an architect. But someone tell me quick, what's the name of the most famous American architect - a household name?"

"Frank Lloyd Wright," yelled Rick.

"Yes! And what home design is he most known for, to most people?"

"The house with the waterfall in it?" asked a woman sitting to his right.

"Yes. Falling Water. And other homes too, that blend into the landscape, right? Anything else he was known for?"

"Functional spaces?" asked another student.

"That's right. Spaces that reflect not just their external environment, but also the purpose and the lifestyle of those who live inside that space. He was known to design furniture right into the walls. Everything that was needed and nothing that wasn't. Now think about it. What's the most basic thing he had to do, to design those two things?"

Blank faces looked back at him.

"One. You have to define the environment, to discover a design to reflect it, right? You have to know where you are. Two. You have to define the people that live in the space and understand their needs before you can design a functional space for them."

"You'll find, in architecture, and in life too, it's always easiest to begin with defining who you are, where you are and your needs. If you want to create a home with others, you need to define who they are and their unique needs, too."

* * *

*What did Carrie need?*

Manny walked to his new office after class. He could guess, but that was a sure way to be wrong. It had been fifteen years since he had held her. He alone was what she needed then. Obviously, that wasn't true anymore.

It was time to think about the students' needs. In his office, he found an index card and a pen. He had a ritual, on the first day of classes, in a new semester. He wrote *My door is always open, even when it's shut. Text me.* He added his phone number, email and office hours and taped the card to the outside of his door. He stood, looking at it for a minute. Maybe it would be enough for a student that needed it. Would it have been enough for him when he was a freshman?

Maybe not. He had felt so invisible then. Somedays, it had felt like Carrie was the only person who saw him. He walked back to his desk to read the roster of student names he had just met. Veda and Rafael were from out of the country. Others were from far away, too. He would know more about all of them after next class, when he read their essays. He read over the roster several times, matching the words with the faces he had just seen, memorizing their names.

He walked down the hall and stopped at an open door to the office of Guy Katsen, the head of his department. He liked Guy's office. There was something cozy about it. A large framed print of Henry Tanner's *The Banjo Lesson* hung over Guy's desk. Manny loved the power of that simple scene of a black man with his grandson on his knee. You couldn't look at that and see in stereotypes, could you? He should get some artwork for his office.

"Is the apartment okay?" asked Guy. He had a warm smile within his neatly trimmed beard. It was just beginning to gray. Someday he would look a lot like that grandpa in the print above him.

"It's perfect," said Manny and then remembered Emily's initial reaction to it. "Well, my daughter helped add a few decorations. Now, it's perfect."

"I didn't know you had a daughter. Is she adjusting okay to the move?"

"She already lived near here. She lives out on Sandy Hook Gateway National Park with her mom."

There was a flicker of a question in Guy's eyes.

"It was one of the reasons I applied for the position here. I wanted to spend more time with her. Her name is Emily. She's fifteen."

"Oh, I can understand that." Guy pointed to a photo on a bookshelf near Manny. "Those are my two kids. They're in their twenties now, on their own, but I miss them every day."

"Good looking kids. Where are they?"

"Back in New Orleans. I just moved here a year ago.

Kids are special. Changed my whole life, the minute I saw my son being born. "

"Mmm."

*Don't go there, don't ask me.*

"How about you?"

There it was. He could say he wasn't in the delivery room. He could just say, yeah, he knew that feeling.

"I wasn't there. I got a phone call, ten years later."

"Wow! Totally out of the blue?"

"Totally out of the blue."

"That must have been a shock."

"It was a shock, yes," said Manny. "It was one of those hectic days, students in and out of my office between classes, no time to eat."

"And then you got the call."

It never failed. Other men were always deeply interested in his story, wanting details. Women, not so much.

"Time stood still. And same as you, once I saw her, my whole life changed. All I've wanted, ever since I saw her, was to be the best dad ever. And to make up for the lost time. This is my first time living in the same state as her. I'm hoping we'll be able to catch up now."

"Do you have any other kids?" asked Guy.

"I have two nieces, in New Mexico."

He saw the confusion in Guy's eyes.

"But she's my only child. A gift."

"Kids are gifts, that's for sure," said Guy. "I'm glad for you that the job brings you closer to her."

He could sense that Guy meant it.

"Thank you," said Manny. "By the way, during the interview, there was some mention of my having an office out on Sandy Hook? But I've been given an office down the hall here."

Guy grimaced and rubbed his beard.

"I'll know a little more soon, but it might not be until next semester that they have you out there. We have a few partnerships we're doing, working on both historical research and new designs of the structures on the Hook. The key player is Turner Construction Co. You'll probably have an office within their facility. I'm actually in the dark about the details on how the University will interact with them. That direction is coming from higher than me."

"Turner Construction?" said Manny. "I know about Tom Turner. I never met him, but I went to undergrad with his daughter, Rachel."

"Oh, you know Rachel Turner?" Guy looked at him differently, as if that changed something.

"You might know more than me, then," said Guy.

It had been Rachel that had reached out to Manny, about six months ago, to tell him the University had an opening in the architecture department. She hadn't mentioned to him how she knew. She hadn't mentioned that her father's company, where she worked, had formed a partnership with the University.

"No, I don't know anything," said Manny.

Guy's eyes were guarded now, the warmth gone. The application process and the job interview had all happened so quick and smooth, much easier than Manny had imagined it could. Did Rachel make that happen? He could sense Guy wondered the same thing.

Manny stood up. "Thanks Guy," he said, shaking his hand. "I guess we'll both find out soon enough."

Guy smiled, the warmth returning to his eyes.

"I'll let you know as soon as I hear anything."

"Same here," said Manny.

A pawn? Maybe. Nothing new here. He wouldn't let it

bother him. He had played this game before. The secret was to redefine that space on the chessboard they gave you. Make it your own.

Manny walked out Guy's door, more ready than ever to see his Emily and hopefully, see Carrie too.

Cochi was right. Manny realized it, as he drove through the National Park entrance of Sandy Hook, and caught sight of his bare arm in the side-view mirror. Who was he kidding? He had chosen to wear this shirt this morning, knowing that he might see Carrie today. She was probably the reason he was tempted to pull the elastic out of his hair right now, too. It wasn't practical to have his hair blowing around in the strong coastal wind. How the hell could his brother be so right all the time?

This was silly, immature, stupid. He hadn't seen her in years. Three years to be exact. Not since Emily was old enough to put on a plane by herself to spend the summer with him. He had thought he would see Carrie last week when he picked Emily up for his first weekend in New Jersey. But Emily had been too excited to see his new apartment, not show him where she and Carrie lived. If Em didn't invite him in today, he should say something. He should, but would he?

The single road down the center of the narrow peninsula allowed views of the ocean on the right and a river on the left. Someone was windsurfing on the river. He looked back at the beach road just in time to see the lot on the ocean side where he needed to park. He turned quickly. He intended to go straight to see Emily, but the sound and scent of the ocean called him as he opened the truck door. A short trail led over a dune to the beach.

The waves were loud and beautiful. They were so damn pretty. He could watch them all day. He was known to watch pretty things.

***"Stop staring at my boobs, or I'll dump this soda on your head."***

***"So you're one of those Jersey girls I've heard about?"***

***"I'm a Jersey girl, but I'm like nothing you ever heard about."***

*Enough.* He needed to stop thinking about Carrie.

He stepped back slowly from the lacey fingers of a crashed wave that reached for him. He looked towards the building where he was supposed to be going.

Emily was waving to him. Over the surf, he heard her calling, "Daddy, Daddy!" She ran towards him, but the sand slowed her steps. He stood for a moment, cherishing the sight of her. Would he ever be so used to seeing her that someday he wouldn't feel this sting in his eyes when he caught sight of her? He couldn't imagine it. He didn't know whether to wish for it or not.

He ran the distance, much quicker than she could. He picked her up and lifted her to the sun. She was tall but thin. They twirled in a dance of pure joy, the sun and pretty waves behind them.

She kissed him and squealed as he let her down.

He laughed. "God, you're getting so big."

"Older – Daddy, older. Not big!"

"That's it. You're looking so old! Like an old lady now."

She punched him playfully. Her eyes were sparkling. He loved those blue eyes, just like her mother's. He stood back, really looking at her. He felt disoriented as if the waves had knocked him over. Last summer, he had convinced himself she was still a kid. But now, there was no denying she was a beautiful fifteen-year-old woman. She had a face full of makeup and a distinct scent of orange candy.

She blew a quick bubble. Not candy. Gum. She was older now.

He tugged her long hair.

"I'm glad you didn't cut it yet," he said.

"You know I'm only joking when I say I'm going to cut my hair."

He didn't know it. How do you tell when a teenager is joking? Shouldn't he know this?

She grabbed his hand and led him towards the building.

"I'm so happy you came today. Is your schedule settled? Am I really going to be able to see you every day, even after the summer? I can't believe it! It's like a new life! I'm so happy, Daddy."

"My schedule changes every semester, but I'll see you every day, if you want, Emmie. It's a new life for both of us."

She squeezed his hand. "For Mom too. It's going to be a new life for ALL of us."

He smiled for her, suppressing the thought of Carrie. He looked up in surprise as they came closer to the building.

"What is this?"

"It's where Mom works. She told me to bring you in. She was mad she didn't get to see you last time."

Carrie mad about not seeing him? Don't get excited. Emily exaggerates.

"But what is this building?"

"Oh, I don't know. One of the old bunkers or something from when there was an Army Fort here. It was camouflaged into the sand so the Germans couldn't see it in WWII, while it protected New York Harbor. Now it's the local Arts Council building. We get to live in the cottage out back since Mom runs the County Arts Program."

The outside of the concrete building was set into a hill of sand directly on the beach and covered in a bright mural. Two mermaids swam with horseshoe crabs, whales, lobsters and more sea creatures. He recognized Carrie's distinct style.

They entered the building into a large space full of tables, easels, paints, rags, and brushes. Canvases and drawings stood in various stages of completion.

"This is where Mom runs the classes."

Manny inhaled the smell of turpentine. That smell always reminded him of art school, of meeting Carrie, of being with Carrie. Did Carrie still work in oils? He thought everyone used acrylics now.

The sunlight surprised him. The low concrete profile of the building on the waterfront expanded into a wall of windows on the western side.

"I love this place," he said. "There's so much light here. I need to take a class."

"I thought you taught Mom how to paint," said Emily, moving towards another door.

"I never taught your mother anything. Believe me."

He looked around, impressed by the vast creative space. He remembered now. Emily had sent him a link to a newspaper article. Carrie had made this space happen. She was a force in the local artist community.

"Where is she?"

"Probably in her private studio. Over here."

He followed Emily through a long hallway. They passed several doors with frosted pane windows, closing off what were once offices and classrooms for the Army. Now, he had read, under Carrie's direction, they were transformed into spaces for creativity and art.

As they entered a large room, Carrie's back was to them. She was pushing a brayer over a large canvas. It was wet with an intense midnight blue. Acrylics. There was no smell of turpentine in here. He was sure she had custom mixed that dark blue. She was using it to highlight a vibrant, textured collage of swirls and circles. An abstract work, it was just beginning to show it's character.

The silhouette of her body against the sun mesmerized him. If he were still a painter, he would paint this scene.

"A masterpiece," he said.

She spun around. He couldn't see her face as she walked to him. The sun blinded his eyes, but he smiled and trusted, uncertain as he was. She stopped dead in front of him and blocked the light. He saw the clear blue eyes.

"Beautiful," he said softly.

She smirked. "Hi, Manny. I hope you know what you're in for."

"I don't have a clue."

"You got that right."

Cut to the truth, no BS. That was Carrie.

She untied her painting apron, lifting the top string through her long hair. His eyes lingered on a single curl dancing in the strong sunlight near her breast. He had an urge to hold her and kiss her in this pure sun. He wanted to touch that strand of hair, lose himself in caressing her, become part of that blue canvas, that raging ocean of swirls. She shook her hair. The curl settled on her shoulder.

"So, where exactly are you going to be working and living?" she said. "I've been trying to get the information from Emily, but that's like trying to read in the dark."

He knew what it was like, trying to get information from Emily about her. There were never enough details. They had that in common. But he couldn't tell her that.

He leaned forward just slightly to inhale more of her scent. It was too subtle for perfume. She wouldn't use perfume, would she? She was more natural than that. It must be from her shampoo. A vision of Carrie in the shower covered in shampoo bubbles flashed quickly.

*Calm down, Mr. Bubbles. Just answer the lady.*

He cleared his throat, moved his eyes from her hair to her eyes.

"I'm going to be teaching at McCauley University for at least a year, including this summer semester. They've given me an office on the campus and an apartment nearby. But I'm going to have an office out here on the Hook too, I think. They have some projects going on out here. I don't know too much about it yet. I was just happy to take the job when I realized where it was, so close to you two."

"Yeah." She wasn't smiling anymore. "A lot of groups have a lot of projects in the works out here on the Hook. The Feds have opened it up to everybody."

He sensed the displeasure. She was opposed to it, whatever the University was doing - whatever it was he'd be doing. Great.

He watched her turn to look at Emily, and he followed

her gaze. Their daughter was frowning. Then she sighed, as only a 15-year-old teenage girl taking weekly acting lessons could sigh. It was loud, dramatic and her whole body was a part of it. Her long, straight black hair shook, and the eyelids above her clear blue eyes fluttered. She threw both hands in the air.

"You two are pathetic! How could you ever have been together? No kiss? No hug? Not even a handshake! Where did I even come from? A test tube or something?"

He laughed and heard Carrie's laugh join his. He looked into Carrie's eyes as she turned back to him, and he could see the young woman who once loved him. She had once seen the best in him. He reached to her. They hugged, a warm hug, only long enough, he told himself, to reassure their daughter she came from love. He felt Carrie's body stiffen at first, then soften. Was it only because she shared his goal to reassure Emily?

He pulled back but still held her. "It's good to see you," he said softly. Then he kissed her as lightly as he could, on those lips he had missed. This was just to show Emily.

She kissed him back, full-on, open-mouthed, passionate. He knew she was playing him, was joking with him, but he savored every second. It felt so good to taste her again. The smell of flowers surrounded him. The scent was in her hair. He had been right about the bubbles. He reached his hand into those tresses.

"Alright, alright, enough! You don't have to be gross about it!" yelled Emily, the director.

They both laughed and pulled away.

Despite saying it was gross, Emily looked pleased. She was smiling. Carrie looked pleased too. Her mouth was set in that Mona Lisa smile of hers. Was she pleased with her joke, pleased with his kiss or pleased he was here? What did she need? Did she need more kisses? Manny didn't know. He knew only, more clearly than ever, that he had no clue. But he was determined to find out.

"Let's go to your new apartment, Dad."

Emily was already heading towards the door.

Manny's apartment was a twenty-minute ride down the Ocean Blvd. They passed through several beach towns, each with a unique style of architecture. He loved the variety of house styles you could see in New Jersey. He wondered if he had gone to college anywhere else, would he have ended up teaching Architectural History now?

"Look," he pointed. "There's a whole row of classic Craftsman Bungalows."

"Too small!" said Emily. "I'd rather live in this one."

She pointed to a stucco Spanish Colonial Revival mansion with a red tile roof that looked better suited to California.

"Too big!" said Manny, laughing. "We'd be so lonely in that, just the two of us. And me, by myself, when you're at your Mom's."

"True. We don't want that one. Don't buy that one, Dad."

"Hmm. Okay. You know, we don't need a house, anyway. Home is where family is together."

His family was scattered now. His brothers rode the wind, Cochi in a van, driving venue to venue to sing the blues and Little Bro, well he wasn't exactly sure what Little Bro was doing these days. He drifted from city to city and job to job. His father, of course, was still in Mescalero, with Shannon and the second family.

"Are we going to miss it this year because of your new job?" Emily asked.

He smiled. He knew what she meant. Every year his family all made their way back to Mescalero in July for the Girl's Puberty Rite Ceremony. Together with the cousins, the aunties, the uncles, the elders and the young, it was a celebration of family and of their people. He felt proud that Emily realized that was the real "home" for them.

"I'm not sure of my schedule yet. I'll find out soon. But, even if we get to go, it probably won't be for the whole week, like we've done before. Probably just the four days of the Ceremony, over Fourth of July weekend."

"That sucks."

She said it just as the scenery dramatically changed. This was his new hometown of Long Branch. High rise condominiums and townhomes blocked the view of the ocean.

"This place is so different now," he said. "None of these high-rises were here when I knew your Mom. It was mostly little Cape Cods and Ranches then. The town pulled Eminent Domain and razed them all down."

Emily rolled her eyes. "How long is this lecture going to be?" She pulled a set of earbuds from her pocket.

He laughed. "I'll stop. You're right. I'm just figuring a

topic for a class. Sorry to bore you. But there's a lesson here."

His apartment building was a red brick, two-story rectangle with twenty units. It had escaped the Eminent Domain razing, probably because the University owned it. The black iron railings hinted of construction in the Sixties. There was nothing architecturally interesting about it. Although it was only a block from the beach, his unit was on the west side of the building. His balcony looked out over a parking lot and dumpster.

Emily had declared it all drab when she first saw it and made him take her shopping for home decorations.

Manny opened the door to the apartment.

"What a change, right?" he said. "Definitely not drab anymore."

The gray furniture was transformed by Emily's choice of purple and bright green pillows and curtains. Everywhere he looked now, he saw the bright colors.

"I like it," she said.

"I like it too. It's you. Very you. You've got a strong design voice, Em. Now I get to live in it, even when you're not with me. Thank you."

"You're welcome."

She gave him a look like she was happy to take care of him. That's what it was, wasn't it? The child takes care of the parent.

Her eyes narrowed.

"Dad, sit down here, please," she said, her tone stern as she sat down on the couch. "We need to talk."

He sat down next to her. "Why do I feel like I'm in trouble?"

"Not in trouble. I just feel like we need to talk about something."

"Okay. Shoot." He sat back on a purple pillow. It was Emily time. He never knew what to expect from her.

"You know all those ladies in the stores last week? Dad, they were all over you. It was so annoying."

He closed his eyes a second and sighed. Emily was not a little girl anymore. "They were just being nice."

"They were all flirting!"

She was right. God, he did not want to talk about this.

He flexed his arm. "I've been working out more. They were just flirting at the guns, not at me. They don't know me."

He wanted to brush it off and make her laugh. Her mouth was firm. Where exactly was she going to take this?

"Well, I've been thinking about it. I have an idea that can stop those ladies flirting with you. I think you should wear a wedding ring."

He laughed, shaking his head. "No more wedding rings for me, Em."

"You've got to, to tell them you're off-limits."

He was tempted to tell her that only works in old movies, like the ones he knew she watched. Women flirted with him whether he wore a ring or not. They flirted with him, yet they didn't really see him. It was like he had a Hollywood doppelganger. It was annoying and embarrassing.

What was going on? Was it that she didn't want to share him? That was understandable.

"Listen, Em. I didn't move here to find someone to date. I don't let the flirting get to me. I'm here to spend time with you. I know we haven't had as much time together like other families, but we'll catch up, okay?"

She nodded. "What about Mom? She's single now too."

"I think you've mentioned that before."

"Don't you see? It's perfect timing now!" Her face was lit with excitement. "First, when we found you when I was ten, you were married. Then, by the time you got divorced, she was married. Now, you're here, and you're single, and she's here, and she's single too! It's perfect!"

"So perfect, makes me wonder if someone planned it."

She shook her head and sat up high, more excited. "I didn't plan it, Dad. I'm just observing."

She was so cute. And she was so hopeful about him and Carrie that it hurt.

"One thing you didn't observe, sweet Em."

"What?"

"How do they say it? She's just not that into me."

"That's not true! At least, I don't think it is. She always wants to know all the details about the vacations I take with you. She always asks me what you think when we talk about important stuff. She's never said anything bad about you, like my friend's parents, when they talk about the ex. I think she's into you."

It was nice to hear, but Emily was going down the wrong road with this fantasy.

He took her two hands. "Emily, you're my everything. You're my sunshine, my precious golden girl. My gift from the universe. You know that, right?"

She nodded.

"I took this job and came across the country to spend time with you before you're an adult because these years, I know, they don't come back. Your Mom and I had something special in college. You truly came from a place of love. Don't ever doubt that. But we've both changed since then. We hardly know each other now. We were young then. Look, now I'm an old man."

Emily looked him over and then patted him on the arm, reassuringly. "You look a lot younger than you are, Dad."

He was fine with looking the ancient age of 36.

"Thank you for that. But Em, I didn't come back here to get married to your Mom. She moved on from me before you were even born."

He could see tears starting to well up in Emily's eyes. He shouldn't have been so blunt. He wasn't talking to himself. He was talking to Emily. He just made his daughter cry. Failure Dad.

"Hey, hey." He brushed a falling tear with his thumb and pulled her to him in a big hug. "You knew that, right? You knew I wasn't going to move in with the two of you?"

He could feel her head nodding yes, against his chest.

"I was just hoping. I always dreamed we could be a family."

Family. Home. That was what he'd come here to give her. Or, more honestly, maybe it was what he'd come here to give himself.

Couldn't he and Emily be a family of two, the same way she and Carrie were a family? Emily dared to dream of the three of them together. He could admit it to her that he wanted the same. But that would get her hopes up. That would get his hopes up. God. She was so much braver than him.

He kissed her on her head. "Dreams are powerful. Don't ever stop dreaming."

Two weeks later, with a slam, Carrie slapped a thick swirl of turquoise paint onto a huge new canvas. Next, she brushed it into a mad spiral. This was only the first layer. There would be many more layers. Many more days of having to see Manny, having to watch him smile, having to look at those hands, those hands that once held her.

She slapped more paint onto the canvas. Splat! She liked that. She felt like splattering this feeling. Damn him! Damn herself! She sighed, looking at the turquoise swirls. Could she handle this?

Splat! More paint, more swirls. Of course, she could. She could keep her distance. She could keep her guard up. He wasn't here for her. He was just being a good dad, as good as he could be, considering.

What if she had told him right away? Splat! It didn't matter. The past doesn't change. Splat! The art and the ocean helped her deal with any doubts. No doubting was allowed to the ocean. No doubts allowed in her art. The canvas was full of a swirling blue, and she felt strong. There would be more layers, many more layers - each a reinforcement of the strength of the swirls, each a nuance of texture and light. Life and love are complicated. No doubting, no guilt, just move on.

She stood back to see her progress, breathing heavily.

"Knock, knock," said a familiar voice. She turned around to see her friend Tori.

"That is awesome," said Tori, looking at the canvas.

"I'm just starting it. There's lots more to come."

"Awesome start. So much movement."

"Yeah, I'm pleased with it so far. Hey, I'm ready for a break, this needs to dry before the next layer. What are you doing?"

"I'm looking for lunch."

"Great. Let's go."

They took sandwiches from the kitchen out to a warm spot on the dunes. It was early May and still cool, but the sun was stronger than it had been all winter. If you closed your eyes, you could imagine it was summer. There was a slight scent of dried dune grass baked in the sun. The waves were loud today. Carrie opened her eyes and looked at them.

"Surf's up," she said. "Did you go surfing today?"

"Yeah, I was out this morning," said Tori. "I caught a few. I can't wait till the water warms up and I can ditch the suit."

"Mmm. I'm longing for that, too. A blazing hot summer sun."

Tori looked like summer. Somehow she always had a glowing tan. Her light brown hair had sun-kissed streaks. She always looked so healthy. She was the most athletic person Carrie knew. They were total opposites. Yet, they had always been and would always be Best Friends Forever. She should paint Tori's portrait this summer.

"Well, it's been a few weeks now, right, since Manny came? How's the family reunion going?" asked Tori.

Carrie laughed. "What family? It's all about him and Emily spending time together. I hear he let her decorate his apartment in purple. Poor Manny."

They laughed together.

She sipped her water, enjoying the warm sun on her face. "I have to say I think he's so sweet to her. She sure loves him."

"Are you jealous of that? I mean, you worked so hard, for so long, being a single parent. Then he gets to step in and be so loved?"

Carrie shook her head. "No, honestly, I don't mind. I'm happy that she has him around now. She's wanted this for so long. Plus, it's giving me more time to focus on my artwork. I'm not worried about everything she does now. It's a relief to know she's with him and not some of those guys she was hanging out with."

"What happened to that bunch?"

"Oh, they're still around. I heard her telling them on the phone that she's busy with her dad. I expect it will change now that he's teaching."

"And another month, end of June, she'll be out of school. I guess she's not going to New Mexico this year?"

"No, he's working at the University all summer. So she'll be here, all summer, with nothing to do."

"Uh-oh, trouble ahead," said Tori.

They both laughed and looked out to the waters of the ocean. A lone surfer in the distance was paddling the hori-zon. Carrie wondered what Manny was doing right now. Was he spending a moment watching the ocean too?

"I guess nothing is going to be the same as it was before," said Carrie. "Manny's determined to be a part of her life."

Tori looked at her.

"Do you think he's come to be a part of your life, too?"

"I doubt it. I'm sure he thinks I'm a bitch."

"You say that like being a bitch is a bad thing."

"No. You know what I mean. A selfish bitch is a bad thing."

Tori frowned and put her sandwich down. "You did what you needed to do to survive. For your daughter to survive! I was there. You went through unspeakable - and we won't speak of it - hell. Now, look at you and your beautiful daughter! You're my inspiration, Carrie."

"I wouldn't have gotten through it without you. You're the only one that knows the whole truth, Tori. To everyone else, I'm just the Selfish Bitch."

"Everyone? You mean your family. Not me. You are not selfish, Carrie! No matter what any ignorant person thinks. And remember this - never, ever apologize for *any* choices you made. Anyone that thinks you need to apologize is *wrong* period. Speaking of which - do you think you'll ever tell Manny about what happened?"

"He's never asked me why I didn't let him know about Emily right away."

"And if he asks? Will you tell him?"

"I ask myself that every day now that I see him all the time. I think I've been avoiding spending time with them because of it. I shouldn't be. Emily should see us together. I know that. She wants that. They've asked me a few times to join them. It shouldn't be a big deal to have dinner with them. And the more I push it off, the bigger a deal it becomes."

She was good at catching tears. She knew how to blink and keep them back. She could pounce on them. You just let anger replace that energy. Get angry with Fate. Get angry with the past. Get angry with the world. She knew how to get past tears. You just used them as fuel to get things done. To paint a better canvas. To raise a child.

She started to plan the next layer of the painting.

"If he hasn't asked by now, he probably never will," said Tori, gently.

Carrie nodded.

"You need to ease into it, spending time with him. And I want to meet him. All these years and I've never gotten to meet him. Hey, you should have a party so you can introduce him to everyone."

"A party for Manny? That sounds awkward." Carrie shook her head at the thought.

"Why?"

"He's not my man, Tori. It's not like he's even my friend anymore. Besides, I did that already. I mean, think about it. That summer, after freshman year, when he worked for my grandparent's restaurant; he met all my family and friends then. But, it made him uncomfortable or something. All I know is he ended up leaving a week early that summer. And our relationship was never the same afterward."

"Well, he didn't meet me! I was away on a summer internship. Your stupid brothers probably scared him away, making up stories about you."

"It doesn't matter now," said Carrie. "It's too late."

"I want to meet him," said Tori, pouting. "I deserve to meet him. I've heard enough about him all these years."

Carrie smiled at her friend.

"Yes, you deserve it, my B.F.F. You deserve whatever you want. Hey, maybe he'll come to the Art Show Opening.

We could have an after-party in my cottage and invite him. It would be fun even if he doesn't come."

"Yes!" Tori was excited. "I can bring my homemade Sangria. And we can get Sam to bring wood and make a bonfire."

"Perfect! I'll send you an email tonight with a guest list for us to go over. Now let me get back to work. I want to finish this painting for the show."

* * *

Carrie approached the next layer of paint with a lighter touch. Thin, graceful lines began to glide over the previous splattered bursts. It might all work out. Manny was easy going. He wouldn't ask anything. He would let her hide in her paint. She dribbled and dabbed soft, golden glows now. She stopped and stepped back.

Where had these sweet, gentle lines come from?

She put her brush down.

Fuck. From him.

A circle of blue swirl, like a lover's head bent to the side so slightly, sat waiting for a kiss. She picked the brush up slowly and gently, so gently, highlighted its center with the sun gold paint. She let the tears escape. Let them flow. Why not? Ugh. She hated painting. She hated the Muse that demanded all her time, all her energy, all her truth. Never satisfied. Must she wring every feeling she ever had through a canvas?

Of course. That was the deal with art.

Accept. Continue. She touched the center of another nodding swirl with her brush full of sunlight. This was her prayer, this touching the center of spirals, like a bead on a rosary, she touched it for a moment, then moved to the next.

Carrie climbed the stairs to the second-floor landing. She had watched Emily enter and exit from this door. Still, she felt uncertain. Why? What was wrong with her? The sound of her boots on the metal steps reminded her of something. There had been another second-floor landing, in another town, when he lived off-campus. She felt her face flush, as though she was a damn virgin. Annoyed at herself, she banged loudly on the door.

It opened. Manny's face was there, as open and trusting as the opened door itself. He smiled that sexy smile, the one that cut into her heart. She always wondered if he knew the power of it. Yes, he probably did. How couldn't he? She smiled back, because, well, she couldn't resist him. Still, she stood firmly outside the door. She focused on the feeling of her feet inside her leather boots. She was grounded here, outside. No way was she going in.

"Carrie, it's good to see you. Come on in."

"No, I don't want to disturb you, Manny. I just came to

get Emily. I tried texting her, but she didn't answer. I'll just go wait in the car."

"No, please, come in. She's not here, but she'll be back soon. I've wanted to talk to you alone, anyway. We never get to do that. Please, come in."

She hesitated. She had told herself she wasn't going in there.

He gave her an innocent look, tilted his head slightly and flashed his sexy smile again. He definitely knew the power of that smile.

"I won't bite. And you have to see how Em decorated the place."

She smirked.

"You're right, I've got to see this. Okay. Let me in."

He stepped aside and waved his arm out to show her the space. Her eyes lingered for a moment on that arm. She had an urge to trace her fingers over the shadows of those incredible muscles. She looked back at his face quickly. He still had that smile on his face. His head was tilted so slightly. She imagined painting his lips with a touch of gold paint.

She turned away, walked and concentrated on the furniture. It was easy to see what pieces Emily had added to the décor. Touches of purple and an eye squinting green were everywhere. Carrie peeked into the bedroom.

"Zebra striped sheets? Quite a bachelor pad you have going on here, Manny."

He grinned. "It's Emily's room. I sleep on the pullout couch when she's here."

Carrie looked at the couch. It didn't look comfortable at all.

"We live so close. You can bring her back to my house whenever you need a good night's rest."

"No, it's fine. I sleep better when she's here."

"Really?"

What thoughts kept him awake? Manny lying in bed, unable to sleep? That was an image that would keep her awake.

"Really. I guess it's a Dad thing," he said.

"Yeah? I can understand that."

Stop. Stop thinking of Manny lying in bed. Tossing. No shirt.

She moved into the kitchen. The purple and green curtains, placemats and dishtowels surrounded them.

"Sometimes I feel like I'm on the set of a tween TV show," he admitted, looking around.

"You just need a big, pink, fluffy puppy," said Carrie.

He chuckled.

"Let me make you some tea," he said.

She sat at the table and watched his hand click the knob to light a flame on the gas stove beneath the kettle. His hands, so sure, so strong yet gentle. They had camped together somewhere, once, in the mountains in northern Jersey. She had hated it, unable to relax in such darkness and openness. He had lit a fire with those hands. He had held her tight all night and whispered to her, stories about the stars.

He turned his back to her, getting the tea and mugs from the cabinets. He still wore his hair long but tied it back now. His body was way more man than it was back then. Way more man. What would it be like, to lie next to him again? What stories would he whisper to her now?

She waited. She savored the silence. She had forgotten this, how easy and relaxed she could be with Manny in his silence. He didn't fill the air with unneeded conversation. He just let it be, a space to dream into. She could look, she could hear, she could plan the next painting, wonder about the sunlight. There was room for all of her when she was with him. It was a surprise to remember this, to feel this again. Could it be possible? Could they be friends again? Should she allow herself to want that?

No.

He placed a cup of tea in front of her. She stirred honey into it, watching the gold melt. Now he was the one watching her hands as he sat down across from her.

"I have to tell you," he said, still watching her hands. "I took the job here for more than one reason. The main reason, of course, is to get a chance to be with Emily more, while she's still in school, while I still have the chance."

He glanced up at her face, then down again. He looked nervous.

"The other reason is, I'm hoping, is so we can address parts of our relationship, you and I. Talk about those things that were left hanging, left unsaid."

She stopped stirring. "What relationship? It's been a long time. We've both had a lot happen in our lives since the last time we were alone together, Manny."

Instantly, she wished she hadn't mentioned the last time they were alone. She saw the flicker in his eyes. They both knew what had happened then. Emily.

Manny just looked at her, speaking without words. She looked down at the tea steam. He knew her. He saw her. There was never any hiding from Manny.

Talk. He said talk. Just talk, bitch.

"Okay," she said. "You're right. We need to figure something out, going forward, sharing our time with Emily and.." She stopped in mid-sentence. Why was he looking at her like that?

He spoke, but it wasn't in English.

"Slow down, don't start speaking Apache now. I've forgotten it," she said.

"I never knew you learned it," he smiled.

He had always teased her of her pronunciation of the few words and phrases he had taught her.

"I knew enough," she said.

He grinned, and then she remembered, too, that sometimes there was no need to know the meaning of the words. Sometimes, it was enough to trust him and to let him make love to her. No, that wasn't what she wanted him to remember. It wasn't what she wanted to remember. She felt warm. Damn him.

"What is it that you want to talk about, Manny?"

"I want to apologize to you."

You can't apologize for not loving someone. She shook her head, shaking that memory of sadness.

"No. No apologies. I'm the one that didn't tell you."

"But I left you. I must have left you feeling like you couldn't tell me about Emily. I thought we were just saying goodbye, at our graduation, for a little while. I thought I'd get that next degree and see you again, down the road. It never crossed my mind there might be an Emily."

He had tried to stay in touch. Did he not remember that he had called and she made her mom say she wasn't home? Did he not remember two letters and three postcards he had sent, that she had read a million times? He must remember she had never answered him.

"No matter what," he said, "I'm so thankful for the time I have with her now, Carrie. But knowing that you felt like you couldn't tell me right away, that you went through having a child, being a single mom, for so long, alone. That kills me inside. That I let you down."

His dark eyes looked so sad. She hadn't only hurt him.

She had made him feel guilty as well. Why had she never realized he'd feel guilty?

"Manny, do not blame yourself. You can't blame yourself. You have nothing to apologize about. We used birth control. It wasn't your fault it didn't work. Look, I know I need to tell you more, but..."

She stopped to think what that would mean, to tell him everything.

He reached out and squeezed her hand firmly.

"It's okay. I don't need that. I'm more than thankful for what you've given me. Emily's my everything."

His touch. His forgiveness. At this moment, she had both. She stared at his hand, holding hers.

He let go. He probably thought she wanted that.

He looked lonely, sitting there by himself, on the other side of the table. She didn't want him to be lonely. At least she had given him Emily. Emily could hug him. She could hug Emily and Emily could hug him.

"Emily's my everything, too," she said.

She probably looked as lonely as him, sitting on this side of the table. They were like two moons that spun around planet Emily. Two moons, spinning, passing each other, once or twice a day. It felt both beautiful and unbearable as he stared at her and she stared back.

Emily burst through the door.

"Hi, Mom," said Emily. Her precious daughter had a beautiful beaming smile that quickly redirected to Manny. Carrie caught it. There was something just a little off tilt in Emily's voice. That smile, between the two of them, it hinted of some plan. Conspirators? She'd been set up.

She looked quickly at Manny. She was sure it wasn't his idea. It was okay. Emily was just being Emily, ready to direct the world in her little play.

Carrie stood up quickly.

"Before we go, Manny, I want to invite you to my Art Show this Saturday at the Center and an after-party at the cottage. All the locals will be there and all my friends that have been helping me raise Emmie."

"Then I'll be there," he said.

"Bye, Dad," said Emily, giving him a big hug. He kissed the top of her head.

Carrie smiled at the sight of the two of them. They needed each other. They had each other now. Manny wasn't lonely.

Still holding Emily, Manny leaned over to Carrie and gently kissed her cheek.

"See you soon, both of you," he said.

Carrie felt a chill. It was almost as if they were a family.

* * *

That night, it was hard for Carrie to not think about Manny, as she laid in bed, watching the clock. It had been so easy to talk to him and to laugh with him. It had been so easy to feel his touch. But she must resist. He was like a mirror that she didn't want to look into. She didn't want to see the young version of herself, the one who had loved him. She didn't want to feel like that young version of herself, the one he had rejected. She was stronger than that now.

And yet, it had been today. He had placed his hand over hers. It had been today, he had looked into her soul, while she stirred her tea. He had kissed her lightly, on the cheek, as if she didn't need thousands more of those tiny kisses covering her body. She didn't need his strong hands touching her. She didn't need him to speak without words to her, reaching for her. She didn't need his hard body above her; his lips whispering her name. She didn't need him.

Ugh! She needed something. She got up out of bed and locked the bedroom door. She turned the radio on low. She felt desperate. No, she didn't need him. No, she didn't need him, but she wanted him. She wanted his body, warm, over hers, like the blanket. She wanted him. She wanted him, so hard against her. She wanted him. She wanted him inside of her. She didn't need him. She just wanted him, to never stop, to keep on going, keep on, until, until, until she was released. Released to dream inside his love.

She sighed, so tired. She held the pillow, dreaming it offered the shelter of his back.

anny was starving after a workout at the University gym. He picked up a tray at the cafeteria just as his phone buzzed.

Carrie. The picture on his phone of her was so pretty. He pushed the accept button quickly. Someone slammed a tray on the metal bars next to him. He could barely hear her. Why hadn't he waited and called her back?

"... I just picked your daughter up from school."

There was a toughness in her voice today that put him on guard. That phrase, 'your daughter' did not sound promising.

"Is she okay?"

"She's okay. But you should see the other guy."

"What?"

"She was in a fight. Well, not really a fight. She punched a kid in the face without warning. Knocked him down. She said you told her to do it!"

"Wait. What? I.."

"He called her Pocahontas, and she decked him in an

assembly when the whole school, all the teachers, the principal, everyone could see."

He laughed.

"Manny!"

He could hear the disappointment in her voice.

"Did you really tell her to do that? You of all people?" she said.

Of course, he hadn't told Emily to do that. Did he need to answer that? Why was this line so slow? There was a hold up ahead where the hot meals were dished out.

"What do you mean of all people?"

"It's just, really? Every time I ever saw you confronted, you'd walk away. Like you didn't even hear. You're usually so passive. I didn't think you were going to encourage her to be violent."

"Passive?" That's how she saw him? Damn.

A student on his left reached over Manny's tray for a banana. Now Manny was holding up the line. He grabbed an apple and moved along.

"Wait, when you saw me confronted? When was that? I don't remember that when we were together."

"No? Well, that makes sense. It's not that you acted like you didn't hear, you actually did not hear. You were too busy looking at my boobs."

"Hey." That's how she saw him, too?

A cafeteria lady stared at him with a ladle in her hand. She did not look pleased. Don't call her 'hey'. He slid his tray quickly past.

Carrie might be right. Art School Manny was obsessed with observing every detail of the way Carrie filled her tight scoop neck tops. She didn't wear a bra then. Her nipples were always hard and distinct, prominent beneath the fabric, just waiting to be touched. He certainly remembered that. Was it good that she remembered that too?

He grabbed a sandwich, any sandwich, and moved to the cashier line.

"What did you tell her, Manny?"

"It came up, yeah. We talked about it, in the car, when I was driving her back to your place last night."

He remembered he had a feeling that maybe Emily had asked too lightly, too late in their whole day together. Like it was something she had wanted to talk about all day, and finally, with just a few minutes left together, she blurted it out. Why hadn't he trusted that instinct, pulled over and taken his time to discuss it with her?

"Emily asked me what she should do if someone calls her that. I told her she had to choose her battles," he added.

The line was not moving at all. Three cashiers and none of the lines were moving. How many people, exactly, were listening to him?

"I told her most people say it from ignorance, some don't, but regardless, she doesn't owe anybody her time or energy to educate them. Our people have already given enough."

He lowered his voice. "I also told her the best thing, usually, is to walk away."

"Usually?"

"There are times when it's not, Carrie. It's a personal choice, each time."

A young black student on the line next to him, staring ahead, was nodding to music. He turned and looked at Manny and nodded deep. No pods. Manny nodded back.

"Okay," said Carrie. "Let's start again. The only thing that I know is that I don't know how to deal with this.

Native issues are your department. Maybe you should be the one to deal with the school for this. "

"Okay. I can do that."

She was trusting him to do that. That was something. Good. Co-Parenting 101. Trust each other.

"There's a meeting tomorrow at 8 am with the principal. Can you go to it with Emily?"

"Will you be there?" said Manny.

The cashier raised her eyebrows slightly and smiled. Cash would be too complicated. He gave her a credit card but smiled too.

"Do you need me there?" said Carrie.

What he needed was for everyone to stop listening to him. He signed the screen and tried to ignore those around him.

"It would be good to be there together, right? To show we both agree? That we're partners, raising her?"

The cashier looked sympathetic, handing him the receipt. She nodded, yes.

"I don't know about agreeing. But I'll be there. I'll be your backup."

"Good," he said and gave the cashier a thumbs up just as Carrie hung up.

* * *

Emily stood up when Manny entered the waiting room outside the Principal's office.

"It was a teachable moment, Dad! I recognized it right away, and I thought, no, I'm not walking away! I'm ready to help all these people learn something new today. I did it, Dad. I made the decision on what I could handle that day."

He nodded several times, once at Carrie sitting nearby, to say hello.

"Okay, Em. So you thought it through, didn't just react. That's good. But throwing the first punch, Em, that isn't acceptable, especially in school. I don't want to second guess you, but you punched someone in the face. That's serious."

"It was just Johnny. He's my best friend. He thought it was funny as hell. I didn't punch hard. It's what I learned in acting class. He helps me practice. He had a fake blood capsule that he broke in his mouth to make it look worse."

"What?" Carrie's voice joined Manny's voice. He looked at Carrie, surprised she was surprised.

Carrie frowned at Emily. "A blood capsule? Really? Then you two *did* plan it."

"No, I swear. Johnny always has one in his pocket. He slipped it in his mouth right after."

This was way too confusing.

"He's your friend, and he called you Pocahontas?" asked Manny.

"That's his nickname for me, since before you told me what it meant. I always tell him to stop but then I laugh. So he doesn't realize how it really does upset me. This time I saw where we were, that it would force everyone in the auditorium to get a teachable moment, including him. I mean, come on, Dad. Not just the kids, but the teachers and the principal too! Now you get to tell them all the history stuff they don't know!"

She was so proud of herself. She was so excited.

He gave her a fist bump. "Little Warrior. Remind me to buy you some t-shirts."

"Yes!"

He looked at Carrie for support. She wasn't giving him

anything. Her lips were glossy and set firm. She wore a green scoop neck dress that contrasted perfectly in tone with her light brown hair. A large silver necklace sat on her chest like a shield. She was definitely wearing a bra. She looked beautiful and untouchable.

"Wait," he looked back at Emmie. "I get to tell them history stuff? What?"

"Or you can do a fancy dance. You like to fancy dance, right?"

He rubbed his forehead into both hands, trying to hold up his head. "Wait."

"I told Mrs. Jackson that I wasn't sure. When we were discussing an awareness assembly if you would fancy dance or not."

Slow down. One thing at a time.

"Emmie, I'm not the person to teach the real story of Mataoka. That should be someone from her people."

"Will you fancy dance, at least?"

"I don't have the regalia here, Em. I'm not sure this is the place to do it anyway."

Carrie's hand was covering her mouth. Being able to laugh with her would be nice.

He looked around the waiting room. It felt familiar. The last time he'd been in a waiting room for the principal had not been a good day. Those were never good days.

"Have you been talking to Uncle Cochi?"

"Sure."

"Sure?" That was way too quick and innocent. What had that brother of his been telling her? "Hmm. Every time I've ever been sent to the principal, Cochi was behind it. Every single time."

The door opened. They were called inside by Mrs. Jackson. Manny entered, recognizing an old familiar feeling inside from the days he had to cover up for his kid brother. Dread.

"I'm sure you've been told, Mr. Allen? Your daughter punched a student in the face yesterday."

Your daughter. There it was again. And who was Mr. Allen?

"My last name is Chattoche. Emily has her mom's name. I heard he provoked her? That he called her Pocahontas? And that he's a friend?"

"That doesn't matter. Physical violence is not allowed in any form, for any reason, in our school. Luckily for Emily, the guardian of the boy won't be pressing charges. We will be giving her detention this Saturday. Normally, we'd have her suspended, but Johnny Frank, the victim, is so adamant that it wasn't her fault. He did, apparently, make it look worse than it was. And his mother, um, his guardian, doesn't wish to pursue this. But we feel strongly that the students should be able to learn from this."

"It's a teachable moment," said Emily.

"Yes, a teachable moment," said Mrs. Jackson. "I hear you're a professor. And you might be able to run an informative assembly for our school, about your Native American culture?"

"There's no such thing as Native American culture," said Emily.

Mrs. Jackson looked at her and then him, puzzled.

"I'm a professor, yes, and a licensed architect. I mostly teach historical architecture and art appreciation."

"But you are Native American, aren't you?"

"Apache!" Emily yelled a little too loudly. "He's Apache. I'm Apache. Chiricahua Apache."

"Em." Carrie said it quietly and put her finger to her lips.

Manny sighed. Why hadn't he introduced himself to Mrs. Jackson the proper way? This whole meeting had started wrong. It felt out of control.

"I think there's been some miscommunication," said Carrie, putting her hand on his arm at the same time glaring Emily to remain silent. She squeezed his arm. Her signal to him to be quiet, too, or a sign of solidarity? Whatever it was, he'd take it.

"I'm sure you understand Mrs. Jackson. Emily is dealing with her dad coming to live here. She's so excited about it and wants everyone to meet him. But he just got here. He has a new job at McCauley University. He needs to focus on that right now. I don't think he has time in his schedule to put together an event for you. "

They all looked at him.

"Right, Manny? You're busy teaching the summer session now, right?"

Emily had only a week left of school. Surely, Mrs. Jackson meant an assembly in the Fall.

"I don't know my exact schedule yet."

Carrie closed her eyes briefly, then looked back at Mrs. Jackson.

"You see, he hasn't even had a chance to fully check-in with his new employer. He can't schedule anything with you right now. I'm sure you understand?"

"Yes, of course, I understand that. I know how much work is involved, teaching in a new place. Probably tons of work waiting for you."

He nodded. There was no sense in trying to explain how his schedule differed every semester. Carrie thought he needed help and was taking charge. No reason to stop her and add to the confusion.

"In fact, he actually has to get there soon, to check-in, right, Manny?"

She squeezed his arm and he nodded. Keep on squeezing, Carrie. He looked at her profile, so close, as she spoke. She was animated when she took charge. Focused. Driven. Passionate.

"...and I have an art class to teach this morning, Mrs. Jackson. We need to say goodbye if that's all?"

"Yes, yes, I understand. That's all."

They all stood up.

Emily frowned and blocked them from leaving the room.

"Are you going to work today, Dad? I thought you were going to pick me up after school? And what about having an assembly that everyone can learn from? I talked Mrs. Jackson into that."

He put his hand on her shoulder.

"Yes, I'm going to work, but I'll be out in time to pick you up. It's awesome that you and Mrs. Jackson figured an assembly for the school. Thank you, Mrs. Jackson, for going along with that. I'll show Emily over the summer how to contact the right people for an event here so that everyone can learn. And I'll take care of the costs of it, as part of my gratitude and to make sure it happens."

"That's wonderful, Mr. Allen. Thank you."

He nodded to Mrs. Jackson, even if she didn't know his name. Even if she didn't know it was her job, not his, to educate these kids. Emily went off to class. Carrie had her hand on his arm and was leading him, quickly, across the entrance of the school. Only when they were in the parking lot did she let go.

"We were a team there," he said. He hoped she saw it that way.

"I hope I didn't overstep. I wasn't sure what you wanted to say. You were taking a little too long to get it out."

Slow. Add slow to the list. Passive, breast-obsessed and slow.

"No, it's alright. We'll get Mataoka's people to come talk, that's what's important. Being called to the principal's office stirred up some bad memories for me. I lost my voice. Thanks for taking over."

Carrie smiled gently. "I remember when Em was in kindergarten, just a teacher conference would give me anxiety. But I got used to it. It's different when you're the parent."

"You've been doing it a long time," he said.

"Longer than you, yeah."

There it was. The Missing Years. It hung between them, like an invisible bridge, they'd never cross.

She must have seen that touch of sadness he felt. Still smiling gently, she touched his arm. "Don't worry. It gets easier."

She was all about touching this morning.

"Carrie, I might not have explained myself well the other night, to Emmie. I should have taken more time with her."

She shook her head and put her hand on his arm again. "It's okay. We got it covered today. Every day there's a new drama with Emily, a new opportunity to say what you think is the right thing. They'll be plenty more chances."

She turned to her car. He opened the door for her, shutting it while she buckled up. He leaned into the open window. He couldn't help but look into that scoop neck dress. She didn't look so untouchable now.

"Who's Mataoka?" she asked.

It surprised him. How did she not know? He shouldn't be surprised.

"Some say that's her real name, not Pocahontas. She was a child, younger than Emmie. She was kidnaped and raped, then taken to England and paraded around like a curiosity. Her people have been asking for hundreds of years for her bones to be returned. They're still asking."

"I thought that she wanted to go?"

"Her people tell a different story."

"So calling Emmie Pocahontas is an insult because ..."

"It's a slur. It's a name for a kidnapped rape victim."

"Wow," she said. "I thought you and Emily were just upset because Pocahontas wasn't Apache. That calling Emily that lumps all Natives together."

"That too, but it doesn't matter what Nation you're from. It always sounds cruel and disgusting. I don't want anyone calling my daughter that. I need to meet this Johnny."

"Oh, you will. I doubt he meant it like that, though. He really is her best friend. I wouldn't be surprised if they planned the whole act. They have a history of finding drama together."

There would be more drama to look forward to. Manny felt exhausted.

"I don't know how you've done this, all these years," he said, stepping back.

"It's easy when there's no choice," she said with a small smile, then waved slightly and drove away.

He frowned, watching the car leave the lot. He felt sure she didn't see him in her rearview mirror. No, he wasn't invisible to her, but still, she didn't really see him. She saw someone else, entirely - some slow, passive guy.

He climbed into his truck and turned the key.

*Apache! Chiricahua Apache!* Emily had yelled it. That was something.

Yes. He scrolled the playlist and the music came on with a boom.

Today was a good day. Emily was in it, teaching lessons.

Carrie looked over the gallery, amazed at the large crowd that came for the art show opening. Every year this show seemed to get bigger.

Tori walked over to Carrie.

"You did not tell me how gorgeous he is! All these years, you never thought to mention he's a drop-dead sex hunk I-don't-even-have-words-to-describe-man-person?"

"Shhh...someone will hear you! He'll hear you! You've seen pictures."

"Those were Dad pictures, taken by Emily. What kind of BFF are you, anyway? How did you not bother to let me know?"

"He wasn't that..uh..that. He was just a skinny kid with a big smile when we went to college. He really matured since then. I haven't actually seen him the past few years, only talked on the phone. I think he's been working out. Right? You think?"

Tori looked at her like she had two heads.

"Uh. Yeah! He's working out with something. Who is

that woman talking to him? She's been talking to him since I first saw him. Do you know her?"

Carrie discreetly looked in Manny's direction.

"That's Rachel Turner. Don't you remember her? We went to high school with her."

"Oh, it is? She looks different. She was a natural blonde, wasn't she? Why does she have black hair now?"

"I don't know, Tori. Why do I see pink and purple in your hair tonight?"

"Because I'm channeling my mermaid obviously, but point taken. Anyway, I haven't seen her in years. Why is she all over him?"

"She knows him from college days. She went to Rutgers too. She was dating my brother Paul and working as a waitress in the restaurant the same summer Manny worked there. So, they must be catching up."

"Did he invite her here?"

"I don't think so. Emily claims she's stalking him."

"Really?" Tori laughed. "Hmm. This is interesting. Should we do something about that?"

Carrie looked over again and caught Manny's eyes. He signaled slightly, a cry for help.

She smirked.

"No. We shouldn't do anything. Let him take care of himself. Here, help me move these appetizers to a second tray. We're going to have to start passing them around."

"Hello."

They both looked up to see Manny in front of them. He was looking straight at Carrie.

"Your work is amazing," he said. His eyes were sparkling and he had the biggest smile. He turned to look at Tori.

"Is this, can this be, by any chance, the famous Tori?"

"Yes!" Tori yelled and grabbed him. They both rocked in a huge hug, like old friends, laughing.

"I've heard so much about you! It's so good to finally meet you. Thank you, Tori, for all you've done for Emily. She thinks the world of you."

Tori beamed. Manny was still holding her when Rachel appeared.

"Tori?" said Rachel. "I haven't seen you in forever. You look so good! I can't believe how great you look."

Tori laughed, standing back. "Hi, Rachel. Well, this is like a reunion."

Tori looked at Carrie. Rachel followed her gaze.

"Oh, Carrie, you're here, too? What a surprise!" said Rachel.

"Yes, who would have thought, at her own art show," said Tori, laughing.

"Oh, yes, the art! I'm so impressed, Carrie. Your work has improved so much since college," said Rachel.

Carrie just smirked and took a sip of her drink. Rachel's eyebrows were perfectly plucked, her lips a shiny red gloss and her suit was so cinched and buttoned it was like she'd been poured into a mold. She had always been image-conscious and contrived. Rachel hadn't changed a bit, except for her hair color.

* * *

After the show, Carrie and Tori set up snacks and drinks in the cottage. She introduced Manny to her good friends and neighbors. Everyone welcomed him warmly. She was proud of that. Her friends had helped raise her daughter. This was her village.

Sam, who worked as a Ranger on the Hook, had brought

wood in his pickup and made a big bonfire on the beach, outside the cottage. The crowd of good friends brought their drinks, blankets and beach chairs to talk under the stars, in a circle near the warm fire.

Carrie stood back a bit, smiling to herself. She was glad Tori had suggested the after-party. She was proud of her friends. She was right where she belonged. She crossed her arms and fingered the silk of her vintage caftan. She'd been so lucky to find it at the thrift store this week. It was comfortable and flowed beautifully. It made her feel like an artist from the 1960s. She had completed the look with big hoop earrings and a statement necklace.

Manny walked up to her. She saw his eyes quickly move over her. She knew what he liked. It was the same as what she liked. Natural and comfortable. He looked sexy in his faded jeans and dark t-shirt. His fingers were full of silver rings. She noticed the leather band on his wrist that he always wore. It was a gift Emily had made him years ago.

"This is a perfect setting for a party," he said. He looked at the horizon. "I can't believe we're so close to New York City."

The illuminated skyline of lower Manhattan sparkled on the left horizon above the water.

"Tourists are always surprised with that," she said.

"I guess I'm a tourist."

"Maybe you need a tour."

"I do, actually, if you get a chance. It's been a long time since I've been here. I'm not sure I saw much when I was here before, anyway, besides you and the restaurant kitchen."

"Lucky you, my grandparents sold the restaurant and moved to Florida. I do remember you saying you hoped you'd never see another clam."

"I still feel sick when I hear the words clam chowder. Hangovers and clam chowder do not mix well," he said.

They both laughed.

"I thought I'd see some of your family here tonight. Your brothers, your mother?"

"My mom moved to Florida too. And my brothers all got married. I don't see them a whole lot."

He nodded thoughtfully. "You've been alone."

"No, I have friends. These friends."

She said it too sharply. She didn't want to talk about herself or her family.

"I see you got rid of your stalker," she said.

"Rachel? I guess Emmie told you. I wouldn't call her a stalker, exactly. I don't know. We keep running into her by coincidence."

"Nothing's a coincidence for Rachel. How did she even know you'd be here?"

"Her father, Tom Turner, is running a study out here on the Hook on commercial development. They're looking at renovating the Officer Row houses and some of the other old Fort buildings. She said she was driving by after a meeting at his office and saw the sign for the Art Opening. I wonder, though. Maybe it was just that she saw my truck."

"Or maybe she was all dressed up with no place to go," said Carrie.

Manny laughed and shook his head.

"I know all about Tom Turner," said Carrie. "He wants to make those Officer Row houses into fast-food restaurants and sunglass shops. What I know about Rachel is she'll do anything for her father. She would talk about him non-stop in high school. She drove Tori and me crazy. It was weird. She acted like we should all be so glad he lives in our town.

Anyway, she always has an agenda, Manny. I bet she's after something from you, something more than your good looks."

He laughed. "Lucky, I don't have much more than my good looks."

Carrie felt some concern. Manny was so easy going, Rachel could probably talk him into doing whatever her father needed without Manny realizing it.

"I swear she only dated my brother so she could get the best shifts. He was in charge of scheduling at the restaurant. What are you in charge of out here for the University?"

He took a moment to answer.

"Nothing," he said. "Nothing yet, anyway."

He frowned, then turned and looked over the crowd. He smiled.

"Your friends are good people, Carrie. Everyone has a story about Emily. I'm glad you invited me. And seeing your Art is the best way to catch up with you. Every one of those paintings, all I see is you, your style. It's so strong. It reminds me of Van Gogh."

"My brush strokes aren't so short."

"I'm talking about the energy. The energy is the same."

"Oh, that's just my tormented soul showing."

He looked at her, really looked.

"A fierce, raw truth. You put it out on the canvas. That can't be easy."

No, it wasn't easy. That was an understatement. He understood. That was good. Then why did she feel alarmed at him understanding? Because he was too close? So close, he knew how she thought?

"It does get physical," she said.

She didn't want to talk about the truth. She didn't want to talk about how she put all her feelings into each stroke.

"Those are some huge canvases," he said softly. "It must get exhausting."

She shouldn't say anything more.

"You've inspired me," he said.

"What do you mean? Are you inspired to paint?"

"No. To live! To live with truth and energy, no holding back. That's what I see in your paintings."

He understood what she was trying to do, but no holding back? Really? She felt like she was constantly holding back. Right now, this moment, all she was aware of was her effort to hold back from him. He was standing close to her. His body shielded her from the crowd. It felt like it was just the two of them in a space full of people. His lips, so sensuous, were so close. Was she imagining, or did she really catch his scent once again? It was a musk of sun and sweat and herbs. She had never found another man with that scent that could trigger her so strongly. No holding back? Truth? Maybe he didn't know her so well.

She sipped her cup, but it was empty.

"Can I get you some more?" he asked. "I need to get myself more water."

"You're not drinking the Sangria?"

He shook his head. "I'm driving and I don't drink much anyway."

She remembered his mom had died in a car crash. Someone had been drinking. She couldn't remember who. She felt terrible for forgetting.

"I'm sorry."

He looked puzzled. "It's okay. It's my choice."

"You can use my couch, you know," she said. "It's comfortable. If you want a drink, or just too tired to drive home, please feel free to stay."

"What about Tori? Won't she need your couch?"

He looked towards the crowd. Tori was laughing loudly and stumbling in the circle of chairs.

Carrie laughed. "She's got it covered. Sam is her designated driver tonight."

Manny took her empty cup.

"Thanks. I'll consider that couch, then."

"Wait. I'll go with you," she said. "I should check on things in the kitchen."

The kitchen felt so small. Or was it that Manny just seemed so big? He filled up all the space here. It was so hot in the house after being on the cool sands in the night air. She stood next to him as he poured Sangria into her cup. He poured one for himself, too. So he had made his decision. He'd be staying overnight. He placed her cup next to her on the counter, but she was in no rush to drink it. Why had she told him he should stay the night?

He touched her on the arm gently. She looked at his hand. It was a touch like one would touch an old photograph, a memory, asking nothing, only remembering. His face was near. The shadows on it intrigued her. His lips were so thin on the corners and yet thick. So expressive. How could anyone draw the sensuousness of them? It was only a sprinkle of charcoal dust that defined them. She could, if she was brave enough, allow them to come into her space, that blank paper she held inside her.

She reached to his arm. Only to touch it. Only to move her thumb across the secret strength of his muscle.

So they each only touched each other on the arm. And yet, she felt all her senses condensed at that spot, as he rubbed his finger into her muscle and as she did the same to him. It wasn't a memory. It was now.

His lips came onto hers.

She pulled back, instinctively.

"I'm sorry. So sorry," he said, pulling back too. "I should have asked. I'm sorry. I should go."

"No! Don't go. It's alright!" Why was she yelling? "It's," she said. What was it? It was awkward, that's what it was. "It's just," she tried again. "We don't really know each other anymore."

He didn't even comment. That made it all the more obvious she was just trying to convince herself.

"Hey!" Tori came through the entry. Now there were three of them in the small space. Tori didn't seem to notice the awkwardness in the air.

"Hi Tori," said Manny. "Do you need a ride home?"

"No, Sam said he'd come in to get me. It's getting cold. Everyone's going home now. He's putting the fire out."

"Party's over," said Carrie.

"Party's over," echoed Tori, pouting. "Was it a good party?"

She looked at the two of them, then smiled secretively to Carrie. But it wasn't a secret smile. It was in full view of Manny.

"I wouldn't know," said Carrie. "I'm not a guest."

"Was it a good party, Manny?" Tori was all smiles now. "Manny's the one that decides, Carrie. He's the one we had it for. Did you like the party, Manny?"

"It was a perfect party, Tori."

He was so damn gracious.

"Let me check on Sam," said Carrie.

"I'll go," said Manny. "I can help him."

"Was it a success?" asked Tori when he was barely out the door. Surely he'd heard her.

"You're drunk," said Carrie.

"That doesn't mean you can't answer me."

"I succeeded in making a fool of myself. Was that the goal here?"

"Oh." Tori pouted again. "No, I don't think you were supposed to do that."

Carrie laughed and gave Tori a hug.

"What were we thinking, girlfriend? Come on, let's find Sam and get you home."

* * *

She needed coffee. She needed coffee bad. The sun was pouring into the windows, way too bright and cheerful. Carrie heard no sound of Manny, so she put on a robe and crept into the kitchen, as quiet as possible. She could see the couch from her little kitchen. She tried hard not to stare, but the sight of his bare chest above the sheet, his long black hair hanging down across it, made her gasp. It was just a tiny gasp. She hoped he hadn't heard it. That chest! She turned around and measured the coffee grounds, her hands shaking slightly. There were tattoos on that chest she had never seen. She turned around and took another peek. He was stirring. She looked away again, back to the coffee. Oh, that chest! It needed careful study. There was just so much more of him now. He was so filled out, so much a man. That chest needed to be above her while she studied it. She wanted to feel him against her. She would press her face above his heart.

His hands on her shoulders made her jump and cry out.

He laughed. "Sorry," he said, letting go as she spun around. "I was just going to say good morning."

He stopped smiling when he saw her face. She knew she was staring. She knew she was probably, as Emily would put it, pathetic looking, staring at that broad chest, so close to her, she could smell his scent. Pathetic in her flimsy, old ragged torn lace robe, full of holes. Pathetic, because she knew he could see her nipples beneath the lace. Pathetic because she could not stop her hand from reaching out to trace the lines of his bare tats. His skin was hot. So hot, so warm from sleep.

"A cross inside a circle," she whispered, placing her palm on the large tattoo on his chest. "What does it mean?"

He put his hand over hers. He shook his head slightly to say no and hesitated to speak. "Everything," he barely whispered.

He looked confused. And hot.

"It's okay," she whispered. "Kiss me."

Before the words were finished, he pulled her to him, until she could feel his hardness, until she moaned while she tasted his tongue deep into hers as she looked up, her cheek pressed against his broad chest. Ah, she gasped and kissed him back, this time fully in front of him, her hands reaching to his neck. He put one hand into her hair and kissed her along her jawline, breathing heavy into her ear, nibbling in a tease. His breathing was so ragged, like her own. It was total heaven. She could feel him, smell him, hear his breathing heavy along with her.

His lips were at her ear. He whispered slowly and deliberately. "Where.." He took a breath. "Where is Em?"

"Her bedroom... I think."

She rested her cheek on his hand a moment, as he pulled his body back and looked in her eyes.

"We can't," he mouthed the words.

She barely nodded. She knew he was right.

He glanced at the hallway, where Emily's room was, then gave her another kiss, lightly on her lips. He traced his finger where his lips had been. Neither of them smiled. He turned from her, picked up his shirt and walked towards the bath.

She stood still for a moment, closing her eyes until her breathing returned to normal. Magnetism. That feeling when you hold two magnets and the air between them aches. She felt real physical pain with every step he walked away.

* * *

Breakfast was quiet. Carrie cooked fried eggs, pork roll and toast for the two of them. Manny laughed when he saw the pork roll.

"Only in Jersey," he said. "I haven't had pork roll since..." He stopped suddenly.

"Since the morning after?"

She shouldn't have said that. He looked hurt. Embarrassed. Guilty?

"Since I left Jersey. But I guess you're right. The morning after."

What was she thinking? No way was this going to work out. Nothing to see here, folks. Just move on. She had to move on from him. She had moved on, hadn't she? Apparently not.

Manny sprinkled the salt onto his plate like a ritual, like a prayer, to the four corners. It had been a long time since she'd seen that. Since. Ha. Since the morning after. She should be kinder to him.

"I'm glad you made the move here, Manny. I never expected it. When I first contacted you, I did it because I knew Emily needed you. She was begging me. But, now that you moved here, I can see even more how much she needed you."

"But you didn't need me."

She closed her eyes. He had no idea.

"Needing someone and wanting someone are two different things."

He sipped his coffee and reached his hand across the table.

She looked at his hand, covering hers. How many times had she dreamed of his hands, so strong and yet gentle? But she wasn't going to be able to do this. It had taken her a decade to get over him the first time. She would not subject herself to that again. She would not lose herself in any man, not even Manny. She wanted him, but she didn't need him. She stood up, picked up the plates and put them in the dishwasher.

* * *

She thought he would leave after breakfast, but he didn't seem to be going anywhere on this Sunday morning.

Well, she wasn't going to change her routine for him.

"I'm going on my beach walk now," she said.

"I'll come, too," he said, grabbing his jean jacket.

"I come out to the water and see what treasures are given to me to work with," she said as they walked. "Every day it's different. A shell, a piece of beach glass, feathers, odd bits of iron from shipwrecks or storm thrown piers. I use it all in my art, whatever the water throws to my feet and I think I can use that day."

He walked along, watching her, as she picked up pieces, putting them in a burlap bag she had brought.

"It's good. You use what's given."

"I do. Somethings will inspire a sketch or a painting, but

I also love found art. I'm happy to create with it. Some people don't relate to it, though."

"Some people don't relate to themselves," he said. "With art, it's all about knowing yourself, finding your voice. You're there. You're doing it."

Was he trying to encourage her? She didn't need his encouragement. No, maybe he was just used to doing this. He sounded like a professor. He would be a kind professor. She tried to imagine him in front of a class.

"I'd love to see you teaching," she said.

"It's mostly just lecturing these days, even though I'd rather have the students more involved. You're the one that's teaching technique. Do you have many students?"

"I do. I teach beginners through advanced. We offer a ton of classes. "

"We?"

"There are two other teachers. I manage the building and the program too."

"And you work on your own art every day?"

"Always, that's first."

She imagined lying in bed with him in the morning. He reached for her and she cast his hand aside. "Time to make the art," she'd say. Really? Could she do that? Would art always be first?

They walked further along the beach.

"You were working as a bookkeeper when you first got in touch with me," he said.

"Yeah, it paid the bills. I haven't always been able to live off the art, but I never stopped making it."

"I should have sent you more money. I didn't know it was so expensive to live here. I'm just realizing it now. Jersey is crazy-expensive."

She had never asked him for money. She'd never gone to the State and filed for child support. All she wanted was for Emily to know him. She'd been surprised when he sent the first check.

"It's okay. I didn't mind doing accounting. I actually loved it. It's really cool, Manny, it's like Zen."

He looked at her as if waiting for a punchline.

"It's true! Everything is a plus or a minus, and the total of everything equals zero. I found it very inspiring and mystical."

He laughed. "I find you very inspiring and mystical."

"That's why you're a good man," she said. She hooked her arm into his as they walked further. Why not take him on at least as a friend, again? He was nothing but supportive of her.

"You see me as inspiring and mystical," she said. "Most other people see me as that weird bitch."

"You're an artist. You're a strong woman. And you're different. Some people are threatened by that."

"But you're not. I don't threaten you."

"It's the way I was raised, surrounded by strong women. I learned, always listen to the woman."

She shook her head. He was too perfect. She needed to be very careful. "You weren't always so comfortable with who I am, Manny."

The wind blew cold suddenly. She withdrew her arm from his, to hug herself.

He sighed. He pulled her to him with one arm, cupping her chin in the other.

"Carrie." He waited for her to focus her eyes on him. "I was a mixed-up kid. I didn't know who I was and I was afraid of love. I know who I am now. And I'm not afraid."

"That's what scares me."

He looked at her lips. "I don't want to scare you."

No, not like that. She wasn't scared of him; she was scared of love. She wasn't sure love could allow her to be true to herself and her art, too. She didn't know how to even start to explain that to him.

"Manny, I don't want to hurt Emmie. If she sees us, she's going to get all excited. That's fine, but if it doesn't work out, then she gets hurt with a double whammy. I can't do that to her."

She shouldn't be shifting the excuse only to Emily's wellbeing. She wasn't being honest with him, or to herself.

He was still holding her. He looked around. "I agree. But she's nowhere in sight."

They were at the tip of the Hook, a mile from the cottage where Emily was likely still sleeping in her bed. Manhattan stood like a charcoal sketch in the hazy distance, watching them.

"We can keep it a secret, Carrie, just between the two of us. We can see what happens."

She could feel herself slipping into his logic. As long as they'd be living close by for a few years until Emily went to college, what was the harm, to be friends again? To be lovers again? She would have time to prepare herself, to lose him again. She could do that, right?

"If we do anything, we have to go slow," she said. "Way slow. This is not the past."

He nodded. "Here. Now."

He said it like a spell. Here. Now. With those two words, he centered her. He kissed her, holding her tighter. She reached to hold his shoulders, steadying herself as she swayed. But the swaying - the spinning - was inside. He kept kissing her until everything in her was inside his kiss. At first, it was tinged with the past, a kiss remembered, a kiss that had been missed. Now, it was now. There was no time. There was an absence of time, a lazy kiss that had no urgency for the future, no memory of the past. It was just now, the two of them, beside the sea, with a warm Spring sun shining above them. The sound of surf crashing was a rhythm inside them. She could stay in this kiss forever. He seemed content, too. He wasn't groping her; he wasn't doing anything but kissing her. As though he was savoring it as much as she was. She wasn't afraid inside this kiss. She was happy.

Suddenly, seagulls screeched and swooped around them, causing them both to look to the sky.

"We should head back," she said, thinking of Emily waking.

He smiled, the way lovers smile when they're both satisfied. She smiled back, wondering how long this could last if it had even begun. He took her hand as they turned around.

The waves pounded, receded, pounded, receded, pounded, receded. Manny loved her to the rhythm of the waves, in, out, in, out. Her moans were like the sound of the seagulls drifting in the wind. He felt the cool wind and the hot sun, together. He was sweating. She was lying on her back on the sand. The black rocks of the jetty made a strong wall behind them. The waves were spreading closer. He was so close to the ecstasy. The gulls were screeching, screeching, screeching.

Damn! Manny banged his hand on the sleep button. It was just a dream. The screeching gulls were just the alarm. Damn! He didn't have much time, not enough to finish the dream. He couldn't shake the image, though. He closed his eyes in the shower, let himself dream just a little more. She would feel so good. She would moan, moan and then her body would be shaking. They would ride it together, the waves of heat, ocean, burning sun.

It was true he thought of her as mystical. He was under her spell. It played in his head all day, just those three words. Under her spell. He was totally distracted, and he had a full day of classes to teach.

He became annoyed at himself. He was a professional, not some love-struck teenager. His students were here to learn, and they deserved his attention. He fought himself all day, reigning himself in each time he was distracted. He was exhausted when he got back to his office at 4 pm. He needed to drop off some books, get a very late lunch and get to the final class.

He was in a rush and almost missed it. The little yellow paper fluttered off the door as he opened it. *I was here*, it said. Instead of a signature, there was a moon, a mermaid and a few squiggles of a wave-crest. There was no mistake; it was Carrie. He kissed the paper and put it into his shirt pocket. She was feeling it too. He wasn't in this love-struck world alone today.

Guy walked by in the hallway.

"Hi, Manny, can you stop by my office when you have a few minutes?"

"Sure, I just need to change some books. I'll be right there."

He wondered if Guy had seen him kiss the note. That was an awkward thought.

He knocked on Guy's open door.

"How's everything going, Manny?"

"Good. I'm settling in a bit. Getting to know my way around the campus. The students are much more focused than I expected. I guess you have to be devoted if you're giving up summer vacation in this beach town."

Guy nodded and then frowned. "The classes are going well, then?"

"Yes."

He waited. Guy didn't call him into his office to chat.

"So, you noticed, the classes are small."

"Yes. I appreciate the small sizes. I can see the difference it makes. Where I came from, the classes were immense, and it was always a challenge to give that one on one when it was needed."

Guy nodded. "We do pride ourselves on having a good faculty to student ratio, but, well, the small class size is actually smaller than we had planned. Our department has been shrinking. We just haven't been getting the students in here. I'm not sure why, although I have some opinions. Anyway, we'll have to market it a bit. Maybe plan some events, get more community exposure for freshman and try to get back some of the current students that transferred out of the program. I'll just be frank; your predecessor wasn't well-liked, and neither was mine. That leaves a lot of work for us to improve the department."

Manny nodded his head. No one had mentioned this when they offered him the position. He had taken a cut in pay to come here, and it turned out the cost of living was higher than where he'd been. It probably wouldn't have changed him accepting the job, but still, he wished he had known this before he moved and made a commitment to his daughter. Hopefully, the job would at least last a few years.

"Let me know what I can do, Guy," he said. "I met the Dean of Admissions, Cece Adams, last week. We discussed planning an event together. She had some good ideas for recruitment."

"Yes, she mentioned it to me. This is my official okay on that. Spend as much as you need. It's important. Ah, really important. The registration for your classes next semester is low, Manny. We need you to do whatever you can to bring the numbers up. We don't want to cancel any classes."

"I'll work with CeCe then. Thanks for the heads up, Guy."

"Good. I'll give my assistant the okay to approve whatever you need, resources wise. Thanks for stopping by."

Manny walked back to his office. He knew he had jumped too quickly on this position. He had dropped his usual cautiousness, with his excitement that he could live near Emily.

He believed in getting things done right away. It was too late for lunch, anyway. He walked straight over to the Dean of Admissions office. Cece Adams was still there. She was able to log into the registration records. They could see the exact numbers of students that had registered for his classes.

"Uh oh," he said aloud when he saw the student list.

"This class isn't too bad. Only needs one more student to be a go," she said.

"That's not it. This woman that's registered, Rachel Turner. I know her. I didn't know she was a student, though."

"She's auditing the class, not taking it for credit, but she is paying full tuition," said Cece.

Cece looked at him over her reading glasses. "Do you have a reason you feel she shouldn't be in your class? I could talk to Guy about assigning one of the other professors."

"No, no. It's fine. I don't have a problem with her. We know each other, that's all. "

"And she just wanted to take a class with you?" Cece wasn't going to let it go.

Why did Rachel always seem to appear when he needed something? He needed, right now, some bodies in a classroom, so there she was, her name lit up in the browser, as if she knew. He shrugged. She might be a little odd, but she had always been kind to him. Carrie thought Rachel was looking for something, but obviously, it wasn't a good grade.

"I won't have a problem with her," he said.

* * *

Manny was making dinner the next night when Emily wandered through the kitchen. Her fingers texting, she barely looked at him.

"So Dad, if you were so in love with Mom all through college, what happened? Why didn't you know about me?"

Just like that. No warning. No conversation. It was a good question. He was not the one with the answer. But Emily was waiting for one. She had even looked up from her phone, waiting.

He stirred onions and garlic into the hot oil, taking his time to answer. It's not a big deal. Just tell her what you know.

"We dated mostly in freshman year. We were just friends after that. I changed my major, and we didn't have classes together, like the first year. We didn't see each other, much, after freshman year."

"Then why was I born after you and Mom graduated, like three years later?"

She was smart, his daughter. She tracked details and found the discrepancies. Details mattered.

"Count nine months backward from your birthday, Em. It was the last week of school, the night before we graduated."

Emily stood staring at him, waiting. She was not going to make this easy for him. She knew about sex, about conception. He didn't have to explain that. This was more embarrassing. She was waiting for the why.

He added a chopped green pepper to the pan. She was still waiting, her hands on her hips.

He sighed and shook his head. "We never got over each other. We didn't want to say goodbye."

"You guys sound so pathetic."

He laughed, relieved. Let her think pathetic. Passion was what he remembered. Stupid, clueless passion.

"Mmm. We were pathetic. Your generation is much smarter. It probably wouldn't happen if we were in college today."

Emily looked back at her phone.

"Yeah," she said, texting someone. "You wouldn't have had to say goodbye. And you wouldn't have lost touch for all those years, at least."

He didn't interrupt her texting, to tell her, there had been a way to communicate back then, in those ancient days. It was better she didn't know. Carrie never returned his calls to her mother's home. She had never replied to the letters he had sent.

How long had he tried to reach out to her? Not long enough, obviously. He'd let them all down.

When Carrie called later, he knew he'd have to mention it.

"Emily did the math today. She asked me why she was born after we graduated."

He left out the other question. Why hadn't he known about Emily? Why hadn't she told him sooner?

"That little sneak! She asked me the same thing yesterday."

Had she asked her why she hadn't told him? Had Carrie answered?

"I hope our stories matched up."

"What did you tell her?" asked Carrie.

"I told her we had never gotten over each other and we didn't want to say goodbye. She said we sounded pathetic. What about you?"

"Pretty much the same thing. I told her we were young and stupid and didn't know how to tell each other we were in love. And how happy I was when I realized I was pregnant and would always have a bit of you with me, in her."

They were both silent. He liked knowing she'd been happy. She had wanted his baby. She had never told him that.

"I'm glad you told me to kiss you that night, Carrie."

"I'm glad you came to my room that night."

"We were pretty smart, for being so stupid."

"We were so dumb, we were genius."

"We followed our passion and made our golden girl, our masterpiece, together."

"She's the best thing in my life, Manny."

"Mine too."

He wouldn't ask her. Maybe someday she would tell him on her own when she trusted him, but he didn't need anything more from Carrie. She had given him Emily and Emily was all he needed.

It was Saturday and an unusually hot and humid day for early June. This East Coast humidity felt like a blanket of hot steam that Manny couldn't get off his skin. Shade was no relief here. He needed the soothing water, the calming and cool breeze, and the scent of salt air. He needed Carrie.

When he parked near her cottage, he saw that her car was gone, but he could also see Emily on the beach with her friends. They were laughing and shouting at each other as he approached them.

"And then, did you see the look on her face..." said one. Her friends were rolling with laughter on a beach blanket.

When they saw Manny approaching, they stopped laughing.

"Hi, Dad," said Emily.

The greeting was quick and reserved, not the usual squeal and hug. Carrie had warned him. Teenagers do not like to be seen with their parents. He thought it was different with Em and him, but maybe Carrie was right.

"Hi, Em. Hi, everyone."

The three teenage boys sat up next to her. Which one was Johnny? Emily kept telling him Johnny didn't call her Pocahontas anymore, but Johnny never seemed available to meet him.

"Hey, Professor, I'm Johnny. Emmie told us about you."

Johnny extended his hand. He looked a little nervous, but hey, the kid had spoken up right away. He had dark, scraggly hair, not short or long as if he hadn't decided which way to go with it. There was peach fuzz beneath his nose, a silver hoop in one ear and a suede necklace with charms hanging on it. Manny imagined the look had taken some time in front of a mirror. It was almost painful to imagine.

He looked down to shake Johnny's hand and saw a skull tattoo speckled with bright orange paint. Manny shook it and nodded. Johnny was an artist. He had a tattoo. Maybe he wasn't so bad. He'd try to talk to him alone, later.

"And this is Mike, and this is Dave," said Emily, pointing to the other two.

He shook each of their hands and nodded.

"Emmie, I've been trying to call your Mom, but she isn't answering."

"She went to the grocery store. She probably left her phone at home. She always forgets it."

"Okay. I'm going to take a swim anyway. Mind if I leave my stuff here?"

"It's okay. We're not going anywhere."

Manny threw his keys and wallet down on the blanket, then pulled his t-shirt off.

"Cool tats," said Johnny.

"Whoah," said Dave.

Manny smiled at the kids. They were alright. He threw the shirt on top of his wallet and walked to the water. As he walked away, he heard them.

"Your Dad is so fucking cool!"

"Yeah, god, look at those tats, man."

"I told you," said Emily. "I told you he was worth it."

Manny laughed to himself. Apparently he was worth something.

* * *

He realized why no one was in the water once he reached wet sand. This wasn't California. The water here got warmer during the summer, but in early June it was still too cold to do much swimming. He took a walk down the beach instead. He needed to walk off the tension from work. He hoped he hadn't made the wrong decision to take this job. He wasn't a marketing expert on selling a major to high school students. He didn't know what else this new job would turn out to require. He just wanted peace, balance, harmony, like the sky, surf and sand here.

He picked up a piece of broken sea pottery that jutted out of the sand. He recognized the blue willow pattern. His grandmother had dishes like that.

"Does she have you picking up trash for her now, too?"

He looked up to see Tori in a wetsuit, with a board under her arm.

He laughed. "I guess she does."

Tori took a closer look. "That's a good one. She'll want that."

He looked around. This section of the beach was empty.

"Do you surf alone?"

Tori shrugged.

"It's not my preference, but it's better than dealing with the assholes."

"What assholes?"

She nodded her head down towards the southern surfing beach.

"It's no big deal. They're just jerks. I put up with them if the waves are good enough. Not too much happening today, though. I'm on my way home."

He walked with her to her car.

"Is there anything I can do about them, those assholes?"

"No. It's no big deal. They cut me in line. They wouldn't do it if I had a guy with me. They're just jerks."

"I might know a guy."

She laughed. "Oh yeah? You got a guy? Send him my way."

* * *

Johnny was alone on the blanket sleeping when Manny returned. Or maybe he was pretending to be asleep. Manny saw Emily and the others walking towards a concession stand. He put his shirt on and grabbed his things. Carrie, in the distance, was unloading her car. She looked cool in a light cotton dress and her hair up in a big clip.

He walked up next to her. The trunk was full with large boxes of groceries from a warehouse store.

"I didn't realize you're feeding an army battalion!"

She nodded to the beach. "Four teenagers, it's the same thing."

He carried a stack of boxes as she held open the kitchen door.

"I met them," he said. He opened a plastic container of grapes and helped himself to one.

"What do you think? Do they pass your Dad test?"

"They passed with flying colors."

"Really? How could that be?"

He popped another grape in his mouth. "Because," he smirked. "They think I'm the cool Dad."

She laughed. "What makes you think that?"

"I heard them say it when I walked away."

"Well, don't let it go to your head, cool Dad. One wrong word to them and you'll be knocked off your pedestal. Believe me. I've been there."

"Not going to happen. I'll always be the cool Dad."

"And what about when you see one of them kissing your daughter? What will you do then, cool Dad?"

He frowned. "I'll strangle him. It will be very quick. Then I'll throw him in the ocean."

She laughed, then looked more serious.

"Really though, you need to be prepared. Actually, um, we all need to be prepared. I made a doctor appointment for Emily for next week to go over birth control options with her."

He stopped and waited for more, but Carrie didn't expand. They stood looking at each other, the kitchen island between them. She was right. He wasn't prepared. He needed Emily to stay a child, be his little girl, just a while longer.

"Wait, no." He shook his head.

"I know you don't want to think about it, Manny. But at least one of us has to."

"She's young. She's too young."

"She's not young, and this isn't twenty years ago. Kids today experiment younger. Plus, her friends are older. Johnny's 17, with his own set of wheels."

"But I trust her," he said. "I trust she'll decide the best thing for her."

"And do you trust those friends of hers that you just

met? You trust Pirate Johnny with your daughter's future? With my future?"

"Your future?"

She slammed the refrigerator door closed. "Yes, my future! Who do you think is going to get to take care of a baby? A 16-year-old? I'm asking the doctor to prescribe pills or a patch, something reliable she can use in addition to a condom."

"Don't they mess with hormones? Increase the risk of cancer? She's so young. Maybe you can talk to her about other ways?"

"What other ways? You mean the other ways that we used?"

He was surprised to hear the tinge of anger, or was it hurt in her voice? She said she'd been happy to know she was pregnant. Still, he hadn't been there when she was looking at a changed future, changed because of him.

"I thought we always used something, but I guess I screwed up."

She smiled a tight little smile and spoke a little softer. "You didn't screw up, Manny. We did always use something. It just wasn't reliable."

He should have known that. He did know that. She was looking at him, waiting for something. Words.

"I can agree we need to be sure she knows all the options and can use what she needs," he said. "Beyond that, I don't feel like we should interfere. It's her life."

"What? You don't think we should interfere? That is so easy for you to say. You're a Santa Claus Daddy that buys her whatever she wants. Don't interfere? Don't interfere when Carrie is stuck raising her and her baby? Is that how you want to lay back and let her live the life she wants?"

She was so worked up.

"It sounds like this is not just about her."

"Yes, you're right. I'm thinking about myself, too. I don't care if it sounds selfish. I don't want to take the chance that the next 15 years, I'll be raising another kid. If I can help prevent that, believe me, I will. I love Emmie, I'm thankful for her, but I need a life too."

"I'll help her raise a baby if she has one. I wouldn't mind, getting a chance to do that."

She looked wounded from the words. He hadn't said it to hurt her. The last thing he wanted was to hurt her.

She looked away from him, then up at the ceiling, blinking her eyes.

Her voice was soft. "I'm sorry, Manny. I didn't give you that chance."

"No. I didn't mean it like that. I was talking about Emmie, not us."

She shook her head and smiled, a tight, sad smile. "Whenever we talk about Emmie, we're talking about us."

He wanted to walk across the room. Hold her. But he didn't want to chance that would upset her more.

She folded the last of the boxes from the packages. "Don't worry. I won't force her to take anything she doesn't want. I just have to give her the options so she can make a choice. I can't rely on anyone else, certainly not Johnny, or god-knows-who, to do that."

He nodded. Better to keep any more words inside instead of spilling the wrong ones.

Silently, they both worked at putting the last of the groceries away.

"Let's take a walk on the beach," he said when they finished. He didn't want to talk. He just wanted to walk beside her in the sun with the waves crashing away this tension between them.

"I can't," she said. "I don't have time. I'm going to a meeting soon."

That was his cue, to get out. This had not gone well.

"Okay," he said. He looked at the door, then back at her. "I better go then."

She came to him and touched him on the arm.

"Wait. You can join me if you want. Your girlfriend might be there. Her father is presenting his plans on the redevelopment proposal."

Rachel was the last person he wanted to see but he didn't want to leave Carrie, not like this.

"Sure, I'll go with you. I'm interested in seeing the proposal, too," he said.

He wasn't going to tell Carrie until he knew for sure, but he would probably be working on it soon. It wouldn't hurt to get a jump-start on the plans.

"Good," she said. "It's really important, to Emily and me, you know. I'm hearing rumors that Turner wants to move the Arts building. I probably won't be able to work or live here much longer."

"I didn't know that."

"Hopefully, it's just a rumor. We'll find out tonight." She smiled shyly. "I'm glad you're going to come with me."

"I've got your back," he said.

He meant it, yet he felt like he was telling a lie. Why? Can you tell a lie if you don't know the truth? He didn't know what Rachel and Tom Turner had in mind for him exactly or what they had in mind for the Hook.

He was amazed at Carrie's calm as she sat next to him in his truck, on their way to the meeting. He felt his own adrenaline pumping like a gladiator about to enter an arena.

Carrie bounded up the steps to the Ranger station and pushed open the doors to the large conference room, while Manny trailed behind her. She was ready for a fight.

The familiar faces of her friends quickly surrounded her. Everyone was concerned with the meeting's agenda. She knew they would voice their opposition to any cancellation of the Arts Center if it were on the agenda. She felt strong with the support of this team of locals.

"See, every one of your friends is here. Everyone's got your back," said Manny, sitting down next to Carrie in the second row. He looked around the room."I don't see Tori, though."

"She couldn't get off work," said Carrie.

"Odd, I don't see Rachel, either."

"Aw, poor Manny. Did your stalker quit following you?"

"It's just odd, isn't it, that she's not here for her father's presentation?"

Carrie didn't bother to answer. Rachel's whereabouts were not her concern.

"There's her father," she said to Manny.

Tom Turner stood up and tested his microphone.

Something always bothered Carrie about that man. She wondered how she could explain it to Manny. Tom Turner was a handsome man. His white hair and white teeth were perfect. His deep tan was most likely from time on his yacht in Miami. He smiled easily at those around him. He shook hands and laughed. His well-made clothes were deceptively casual, made to hang perfectly without causing any attention.

Deceptive. That was the word for him.

"I don't trust him," she said to Manny. "I can't even tell you why, exactly, I've just never trusted him."

Manny was studying Turner.

"He looks like he usually gets what he wants," said Manny.

"Yeah, well, not today."

"Tell me, Carrie, why is everyone so sure this redevelopment isn't right for the Hook? Have the details already been released? I thought they still have to do the study."

"It's something we've all lived through before, Manny. We know how this goes. It seems every time a new director is sent here, every ten years or so, he comes up with what he thinks is an original brilliant idea to help the budget. They want to give their responsibility of maintaining all these old buildings over to commercial partners who, in return, will get to use the buildings for their own interests. The locals fight it every time because this is not where we need that. We're in the most densely populated state in the Union. We gave the Feds this land so they would protect it from becoming commercialized. So the locals and the tourists (who we call Bennies) can have a place, just a stone's throw from New York City, to retreat. This isn't like other

National Parks. It's tiny and it's surrounded already by all the commercial businesses that anyone needs. The only thing the Feds have to do is keep it maintained and yet they try to shirk that responsibility every chance they can."

"What do you think Turner's stake is in this?"

"He has a reputation around here of grabbing waterfront property and putting up huge, ugly private houses that take a treasured view away from everyone. I think he only cares about the money he can make."

"Isn't he working for a non-profit here?"

"You think he's doing it for nothing, Manny? If his big-money friends get to move business onto the Hook, do you really think he won't benefit in some way?"

Before Manny could answer, Turner walked back to the microphone.

"Thank you, everyone, for being here," he said. "I'm happy to share with you the details of our proposal for the commercialization of parts of the Park. I'm grateful to the members of the National Park Service here who have put out the call to action requests. Before I begin, I'd like to stress that these points are all proposals only and an informal meeting for the community. The official proposal will be formally presented early this Fall to the planning board of the park and voted on then."

"Lights," he said.

An assistant turned the lights off, and the slides began. Turner wasn't past the third slide before someone yelled out an opposing view. Each slide brought up a discussion, if not an outright round of boos and curses.

"This is a tough crowd," said Manny.

"This crowd is people who work or live on the Hook," Carrie said. "We're not going to let him get away with anything without a fight."

Eventually, the slide of the Arts Center appeared. Carrie sat up straight, her jaw rigid as she stared at Turner. Her hands at her sides were in fists.

"Now, I know some of you have worked hard to make this old bunker into a valuable resource for the arts community," said Turner. "We all appreciate that. It's become a real treasure. We'd like to reward that effort by creating a new building, over here near Officers Row, to house a state of the art media center."

He clicked the next slide to show a nondescript modern style building.

"That's a monster," said Carrie. She stood up and shouted to the room. "Why do we need a new building when we've got 100 historic buildings on this site already, with great spaces and great history, that are falling down? I can understand if you don't want to use the bunker, but there are plenty of other choices. There's no need to build this huge, cold, clueless monstrosity. It will look totally out of place on this site."

Turner looked toward her. "Maybe you're a little too close to the project, Miss Allen. I mean, we all appreciate the effort you've made, but it's time for the professionals to help now."

She glared at Turner, ready to devour him when Manny stood up beside her.

"I'm a professional architect," he said. "I also teach Architectural History at McCauley University. She's right. That design isn't right for this environment. It would be fine for a Mall or a huge corner lot Pharmacy on a highway. It has nothing in common, style-wise, with any of the historical buildings on the Hook. The energy alone to build it, let alone maintain it, would far exceed the costs of renovating, for example, one of the mansions on Officers Row."

"All the mansions on Officers Row are already targeted for other occupants," said Turner, eyeing Manny curiously, as Manny and Carrie sat down.

"For fast-food chains," yelled out Sam. "The traffic for them is going to put the wildlife in danger. Have you ever been out here in the Fall, when the migrating birds are here, when the geese are walking across the road? Have you ever seen the baby turtles crossing the street? We don't need people speeding here to get their fast hamburgers and run over the wildlife."

"I saw a fox last winter," said someone. "I saw him every morning, walking down the road."

"It's fragile," said another. "This is just a fragile spit of beach with one road down the center, and you want to increase the traffic here tenfold throughout the year. Our wildlife and beaches are going to be in danger just so the world gets more hamburgers, french fries, and corporate offices? I don't think so."

"Please, settle down," said Turner. "I'm sure you know, the park has rising costs. It's the only urban National Park in the US. The call to action was to partner with commercial interests to alleviate the high cost of repair and maintenance by renting out these buildings. The renovations will be done without cost to the Park."

"So what, if it will cost us our beaches and our wildlife!" yelled Carrie.

The crowd voiced their agreement.

"The state should never have given this park to the Feds if they can't take care of it," said one man.

"I thought a National Park is preserved for future generations," yelled another.

"I've heard enough," said Carrie, standing. "I'm leaving."

Manny followed her out, and others did the same.

"I don't understand how this happened," said someone.

"It's simple," said Carrie. "The work of maintenance was pushed off to people who are not invested in this land. The decision-makers don't use it like we do. They don't love it like we do. We need to go straight to the source and tell them it's unacceptable."

"You'll probably lose your housing if you make a stink," cautioned Sam.

"Who cares?" said Carrie. "I'll sleep in my car if I have to. I'm not going to let these ignorants wreck the beaches or put up a bunch of McMansions on the one stretch of land that everyone comes to, to get away from all that. Everyone deserves this place untouched. The wildlife deserves it, us locals deserve it, even the Bennies deserve it."

Manny was silent as he drove back to the cottage. Carrie took the time to breathe the salt air slowly. She wasn't upset about losing her housing or the job. She didn't want to lose either of them, but she knew she could take care of herself if she did. She knew this gig wasn't going to last forever, anyway.

What bothered her was the possibility that terrible changes to the Hook itself might be made. She'd seen enough of the local parks redesigned to little more than parking lots in the past few years — someone who cared about more than themselves or their commercial partners needed to be guiding these decisions.

She looked at Manny. He had said he was going to be working out on the Hook soon. She felt hopeful that he could use his role in the University to help mitigate the changes. If anyone could help, it was Manny.

"You were like a Warrior Queen back there in the meeting," said Manny, when they entered the back kitchen door to the cottage. Why did he ever think Carrie might need him? She was capable, all on her own, to take on the world. He had seen that today, in action.

"That's right. Don't mess with me."

She went directly to the refrigerator and pulled out a pitcher of Sangria, asking Manny by lifting her eyebrow if he needed one. She poured them both a tall glass.

"I will never mess with you," he said, taking the drink. "You had me feeling sorry for Tom Turner. That man is going to work hard for whatever it is that motivates him."

"That's a fact. Thanks for sticking up for me on that architectural question, by the way. He looked surprised when you mentioned your credentials."

Manny swallowed. She didn't know. It was likely that Turner knew precisely who he was.

"You were right about the building," he said. "It doesn't take an architect to see that. It's hard for me to believe it will be approved anyway. Local officials have a vote in it, don't they?"

"Yes, but they can only vote on what is presented. And most of those who have a say in this, that are on the Board, don't use the Hook. They go to their private beach clubs further south. If you grow up rich around here, you will think the Hook is just for the poor locals, fishermen and tourists. Maybe they think it's generous to give us more fast food and sunglasses. They don't realize how precious this spit of land is to us."

"Let me know how I can help," said Manny. He sat on the couch and relaxed back into the cushions.

"Well, I need to get involved with a local group that's fighting this - the Clean Beach Committee. I'll let them know you can help if we need any architectural plans reviewed."

"Good. And don't worry about the housing situation. I'm not going to let you sleep in your car."

Carrie laughed. "I'm not worried. I'm a survivor. But thank you. And I'm sorry for yelling at you earlier today when we were talking about Emily."

She stood in front of him, smiling. Her head was tilted so that her long hair glowed in the soft light. She was such a beautiful woman. He pulled her to him. He had to touch her.

"Sit on my lap, then."

She sat down, but instead of sitting sideways, she straddled him. He groaned softly. He wanted her. He knew she knew it.

She reached her arms up to rub behind his neck. "You are tense. Is that all my fault?"

"Not you. Just things. At work."

He laid back into her hands, closing his eyes. "That feels good."

"Did you need me, Manny, is that why you came to see me today?"

"I needed you. I need you, now."

He felt her warm lips on his. He lost himself in her taste.

The kitchen door slammed immediately followed by loud laughter and giggling.

"Teenagers," growled Carrie, pulling away.

"Hey, Mom and Dad," yelled Johnny. "Don't mind us. We're just getting a snack. Just uh, continue on there."

There was more laughter.

"Get out," yelled Carrie, waving her arm.

"We're gone," yelled Dave.

"We're going to movies," yelled Emily, her mouth full of food. "I'll be late."

The back door slammed closed in the midst of their laughter, which grew distant.

"So much for keeping this a secret," said Carrie.

"What time is I'll-be-late?"

"It's Saturday, so it means we have until eleven before we all become pumpkins."

His gaze dropped to her breasts. "I love your pumpkins."

He questioned her with his eyes. She answered by again kissing him deeply, as he touched her, but she quickly pulled back.

"On second thought, I don't trust them," she said. "Come with me."

* * *

She led him by the hand to her bedroom. Manny locked the door behind him, then turned.

She sat on the edge of the bed, slipping off her sandals. She was so beautiful, glowing in the lamplight. Her warm smile welcomed him. The thin cotton dress was fastened by tiny buttons all along the front.

He knelt in front of her.

"So many buttons," he said. He touched the first one. It was impossibly small, sitting between her two breasts. He fingered it, wondering, how could anyone unfasten it. This was going to take a while.

"There's an easier way, Einstein."

She pulled the dress over her head to reveal her creamy skin and a pink bra with black lace. She laid back on the bed.

"Ahhh," he said.

He kissed her on her lips, then slowly, so slowly, down her front. Her skin was so soft, so warm. He pulled his shirt off, to feel his skin on hers. He kissed a freckle here, a little mole there, the familiar marks of her body.

"I missed you."

She sighed. "Manny."

He savored every bit of her skin. He was determined to kiss every inch of her, to show her his adoration. He could take care of her, didn't she know that? He would have to prove it to her. He could feel his own needs fall away, as his only need became seeing her, touching her, hearing her, going to that place of true, natural, primal love. This was love, yes, this was making love. He knew she couldn't get there without trusting him. He knew she couldn't trust him, without his showing her, her total satisfaction was all he wanted.

She held back at first. He could sense it. He could feel

her body not ready to let go, as much as she might want to. He let her take off the bra and then the lace when she was ready. He was gentle, teasing until he sensed her ready for more, bit by bit, he followed her lead and then went on, taking her to new places. When she went there, he could not stop bringing her on and marveled that she did keep going. She was trusting him, holding him, moaning deep inside. His own body was on fire with the sensual beauty of watching her, feeling her, hearing her, tasting her. He was all hers.

He came up to her face and saw tears. He licked the salty water and kissed into her hair, gently.

"You..you brought me way over the edge," she said, running her hands over his back. "How do you know, just what I need?"

"Dreams. You're in my dreams."

She put her arms around his neck and looked into his eyes.

"Come with me, Manny. Come inside me."

Her eyes closed for a second as she said it and her lips were opened, sucking in the pleasure of the thought. He moaned in response, feeling himself hard against her, there where he had tasted her wanting him. He pressed his lips on hers, giving her his tongue, breathing with her.

He wanted to give her all. All he wanted to do was give her his all. He forced himself to stop.

"It's enough for me, just tasting you tonight. We don't have to. I can wait. I don't want to rush loving you."

She glanced at the clock. He let himself look too. Time. Measurements of the sky. Measurements of a night's pleasure. He wanted to let the clock turn until dawn through its circles, but he didn't want Emily to find them in the bedroom when she came back.

Carrie ran her hand down him. He felt her fingers pressing and dancing across him. It wasn't his decision now. He was under her control.

"Let me see you, let me taste you," she said.

He stood up and pulled off the surf shorts, watching her watch him. Her eyes were heavy with the longing. He stood for a minute, letting her see him, letting them both feel the pain of anticipation.

She groaned and moved to the side of the bed. Sitting up, she reached to him, taking hold of him.

Her tongue licked him. He gasped, moving his hands into her hair. It had been so long. He was careful not to guide her. He wanted only what she wanted. She rubbed her breasts against him and he felt weak. Weak and strong. That's how she made him feel. Both weak and strong at the same time. What a woman. She'd found a rhythm that was just what he needed.

He opened his eyes, in wonder just as she stopped suddenly and looked up at him, her lips wet and smirking. He rocked in longing. She smiled and held his cock between her breasts with one hand while she pulled the drawer of the nightstand open with the other.

What was she doing? He was so close. She flicked a foil packet.

"Are you sure?"

"I demand it," she said and laid on her back, tearing the packet open.

He climbed over her, feeling her take hold of him and sliding it onto him. He was all hers. He kissed her breasts.

He turned her beneath him. He wanted to kiss along her back, put his hands on her cheeks, feel...

She groaned and slipped away, twisting back around to face him.

"What?" he asked.

"I need you where I can see you," she whispered. "I need your face in front of me."

"My face ..."

She ran her hands along his face as he entered her. "Your face. So sexy. So good to me. I want to keep you in sight."

She wanted all of him and he would give it to her. Her warmth burned him, made him thrust into the fire, again and again. He could feel the rhythm of their heartbeats, the drum of life. He heard and felt the drums. She was so special to him, this woman. She had given him a daughter. This beautiful woman who allowed him to love her. This woman of fire. She demanded he love her. He was all hers. He could feel her trembling again. This time they would share it. He held longer, like dancing, pushing past exhaustion, pushing to the other place. And when he felt her cresting, he went with her, moaning with her, loving her, all hers.

Manny sat in the chair in Guy's office, with his morning coffee. Guy had asked him to come to his office for a meeting.

"So, we've had a few changes for your Late Summer semester schedule," said Guy. "You'll be working for the Thomas Turner Foundation, out on the Hook, during the day. You'll also have two night classes to teach here on campus. They meet twice a week. I know it's a full schedule. But I hope you'll agree. It's as they say, better than nothing."

Manny looked over the schedule. For most of July and August, he would be working 10 hour days. Not the ideal way to spend a summer at the beach, but Guy was right, better than the alternative. He wanted more than anything to keep this job so close to Emily and Carrie.

"Will I be teaching classes for Turner?"

"No, this is all research. It's covered by our research grants. I believe you'll be working mostly with his daughter, Rachel."

"I thought Tom Turner ran a commercial firm. How does he benefit from the University research grants?"

"He has several organizations. The Thomas Turner Foundation is a non-profit that is in partnership with the University."

"It's a full schedule, Guy, but I'm sure I can handle it. I wish I understood more about how this happened, though, that I'll be researching for Turner."

Guy smoothed his beard, looking down at his desk, then up to Manny.

"Manny, have you ever looked at the name on top of this building? Most people don't notice it. But your answer is right there in granite. The Thomas Turner Foundation. In a nutshell, he's our biggest donor, and he asked for you.

"Don't worry. It should be interesting work. You'll be digging through the old historical plans and matching them to the current condition of the buildings. His preliminary research shows most of them are crumbling and need to come down. You'll be asked to consult with some engineers, verify that for him and present it to the opposition in the community. I hear he got hammered at the last public meeting. I suspect you're the frontman now instead of him."

The frontman for Turner. Manny almost choked on the coffee. He needed out of this.

Manny looked at the schedule again. "Fourth of July weekend. Do I get that off?"

"Sure, it falls between our Early Summer and Late Summer semesters. The University shuts down that whole week."

At least he'd be able to go to New Mexico for the Ceremony.

"Good. Thanks, Guy," said Manny as he left.

His worst fears were coming true. Would he really have

to stand up in front of Carrie and her friends someday to tell them their homes and arts center would soon be demolished? Carrie, he knew, would blow the roof off, without the need of a wrecking crew. He wouldn't mention this to her unless and until he had to.

* * *

Manny saw Rachel walking across the parking lot towards him as he crossed the campus. He held his hand up to wave hello. When she saw him, she suddenly turned direction and headed towards the nearest doorway of a building.

Again, he saw her about an hour later. This time, she didn't see him come up behind her in the hallway of the Admissions building.

"Rachel, hello," he called.

She turned around, looking surprised.

"I noticed you weren't at your father's presentation the other night," he said as he walked up to her. "Are you feeling okay?"

She smiled slightly, looking confused. "I'm okay. I had car trouble."

"Oh, did you get it fixed? I can take a look at it if you want. I know my way around an engine."

"Maybe you should," she said with an odd look. "I'm on my way to my car right now."

Manny forced himself to take small steps as Rachel walked in her high shoes beside him. The cherry trees were in bloom, he noticed. How do women ever get anywhere?

"Manny, I was in the registration office because I decided to withdraw from your class."

Relief.

"I was surprised you were registered in the first place. I think you know the material."

"I wanted a refresher on it. But then I realized Carrie wouldn't understand."

"Carrie?"

Where the hell had she parked, anyway? They had already passed two parking lots. Now they were headed to the overflow lot.

"I don't want her to be jealous of us."

*Us? What the hell?*

"Oh, don't misunderstand me, Manny. We both know there's nothing between us. But Carrie doesn't understand that, does she?"

They turned a corner and now Manny could see the car. Now he knew why she had parked as far from others as she could. Her white sedan was a spray-painted mess. THE STALKER was sprayed in script along one whole side. Stay Away Bitch was on the driver's side door. A stenciled skull was on the trunk. All was done in bright orange spray paint.

"Damn," he said. "That looks like more than car trouble."

"Do you have any idea who would do this?" she said.

He was tempted to ask her who else she was stalking, besides him. But he had a good guess who had done it and it sure wasn't Carrie. And he sure wasn't going to tell Rachel.

"I just moved here. I don't know too many people."

"Carrie works in spray paint, doesn't she? I could swear some of the murals at the Art Show had the same orange paint. I'm glad for Emily's sake you moved here, Manny. I hope you can protect her from Carrie's uncontrollable outbursts. I've heard rumors of them and I know she jumped up yelling in that meeting the other day, but I never thought I'd be the victim of one of them. I'm sorry for what you have to go through, Manny. It must be worse for you."

He shook his head and sighed. There was no reason to explain his relationship with Carrie to Rachel. It was none of her business. Clearly, she knew nothing about it and was creating a story herself. Or repeating gossip? Gossip she had made up, too? This was a mess.

"Well, you can tell Carrie I heard her loud and clear," said Rachel, getting into her car. "I'm not taking the class because I can't afford to get my car vandalized again."

She lowered her window. "But you'll have to tell her, Manny, that you'll be working with me."

Was it that Rachel was telling him what to do that irked him so much, or was it that she was saying what he wouldn't tell himself? It was true that sooner or later, he would have to tell Carrie he was working for Turner.

"I just found out we'll be working together," he said. He put his hand on the car door as he leaned in the window. The paint felt textured. He lifted his hand. There was paint on it.

"Wait," he said. He scratched the paint on the door lightly with his fingernail. It flaked off.

"Do you realize this is temporary paint? You can get this washed off."

"Are you sure?"

Rachel got out of the car to see.

"Oh, that's a relief, at least. I was on my way to the auto body shop to get an estimate for a paint job."

"I think a good car wash with hand detailing will get it off for you."

"Good," she said. "The insurance company will be happy with that. I suppose I should tell the police, too."

"You reported this?"

"Of course."

"Did it happen here on campus?"

"No. It was on the Hook when I was parked at my father's office on Saturday morning."

Rachel got back into her car.

"I had no choice but to report it, Manny."

He watched her drive off while he stood in the parking lot. The spring wind blew cherry blossoms from the flowering trees surrounding the lot. He held his hand out, and a flower landed in his palm. He closed his eyes for a moment. Beauty. But the pretty petals weren't enough to change this day. He had a feeling things were going to get even worse.

Manny had not been home for twenty minutes after his night class when there was a loud banging on his apartment door. Carrie pushed her way inside as soon as he opened it. She stood glaring at him, her hands on her hips.

"Do you have anything you want to tell me?" she asked loudly.

This was not the time to tell her how much he loved her. He knew that much.

"Calm down?"

"No! Wrong! Not calm down! I'm Jersey. I don't do calm!"

He waited, still standing near the door. She paced, threw her purse on his couch, sat down next to it, then got up, and paced some more.

"I heard a story today. Sam came by to tell me. He's buddies with the Police Chief. It was a story about me and your wacky girlfriend. She's accusing me of spray painting her car! And that's not all. She's saying when she confronted you with that, somehow you knew all about it, somehow you knew that it was temporary paint and most importantly, you didn't defend me, you agreed with her, that I'm some uncontrollable bitch."

He stood silent.

"Is any part of that true?"

"Carrie."

"Did you defend me?"

"I didn't say anything to her about you."

"Oh god, Manny, that's just it! You don't say anything! You're so damn passive!"

He closed the door and moved a little closer to her.

"She doesn't deserve an explanation, Carrie. I don't have to answer to her about our relationship."

"She's spreading shit about me in the Arts community, Manny, telling everyone I'm a wacky-assed bitch. I need all the support I can get right now, to keep the Arts Center open. I don't need anyone doubting my capabilities. All you had to do, literally, all you had to do, was speak up for me. Maybe it wouldn't have changed what she's doing, but at least I'd know you had my back. Now. Now, I don't know what to think of you, Manny."

He started to walk towards her.

"Carrie," he said, reaching to her.

She pushed his hands away and shook her head, then picked up her purse.

"Listen. I think we need to take a break from each other. Maybe there's a reason we haven't been together all these years, Manny. Maybe we should think about that a little more. We're going too fast, anyway. We need to slow down."

"Carrie."

"A break. At least," she said, her voice lower. She looked at him for a second and closed the door.

"I don't understand," said Tori.

Carrie was eating lunch with her at an outdoor cafe across the river from the Hook. They were sharing a plate of steamers. Tori dipped her clam into the melted butter and held it in the air.

"One day, you're telling me you and Manny finally made passionate love and next thing I hear, you're saying it's all over?"

She popped the clam into her mouth as Carrie reached for another shell.

"Maybe not over. Just cooling it, at least. What's the rush?"

"What's the rush? Take a look around here. I don't see too many guys that are single, kind, funny, and would do anything for their kid or their woman, not to mention being as easy to look at, as Manny. What are you thinking, girl? What's the rush, it's only been 15 years? Time might be running out. You want him? You better get him while you can."

"Its either too late or it's not. Besides, he's not like that.

He's not going to just run after some tail that shakes in front of him."

"What about an old friend, like Rachel?"

"She's not his type," said Carrie, taking a sip of her drink. She might not always understand Manny, but she knew what turned him on.

"She could be anybody's type, once she knows what he likes. I heard from my realtor friend that Rachel's looking at storefronts in town to open an Art Gallery."

Carrie fingered the ridges on the clamshell. An art gallery felt like an encroachment into her space. What was it with Rachel? She had some type of personality disorder, for sure.

"Ha. I shouldn't be surprised. But Daddy's money can't make her an artist."

Two jetskis broke the quiet river sounds as they zipped past the restaurant. It was a young couple. They were laughing together. Carrie envied them a moment.

"Do you think she wants him, romantically?" said Tori, not even looking at the couple.

"I don't give a shit what Rachel wants, Tori. If Manny wants her, he's welcome to her. I only want Manny if .." She struggled to find the words.

"If what?"

What was it that she wanted from Manny? Was it something she needed from him, or was it something she needed from herself before she could give him her heart? Before she could allow herself to have him?

"What really happened, Carrie? Was he not as good in bed as you remembered?"

Carrie laughed and sipped her drink. "Oh god, Tori. You wouldn't believe how good he is. All he wants to do is take care of me. I had to demand he let me take care of him, too. He is so sweet and sexy."

She thought of Manny loving her.

"Why would you push a man like that away?" said Tori.

"He's too laid back. He didn't say anything to Rachel when she accused me of painting her car. He told me, flat out, he didn't say anything because she didn't deserve an explanation of our relationship - whatever that means."

"So, he had a reason."

"But, he's always like that. He never speaks up."

"But if you're with him, you'll speak up, right? Maybe that's why he likes being with you. He needs that part of you. And you need his calm. You compliment each other. Do you really want a Manny that reacts to everything the same way you do?"

Carrie tried to imagine it. She giggled.

"That could get loud," Carrie admitted.

"And dramatic. I think you have enough drama every day between you and Emily. Do you need a Manny-Opposite adding to it? Just imagine. Three of you in the house, yelling about burnt toast, all waving your arms, like a flock of seagulls fighting about french fries."

They both laughed.

"Okay. You have a good point. Maybe I was a little rough on him. I know I didn't give him much time to explain. But I still think we need to pace this slower. I don't want to repeat what I did with the ex. I need to be sure that I don't give myself away - my interests, my priorities, my friends like you."

"I can understand that. Men don't even know a tenth of what we give to them," said Tori.

"Right. They don't ask for it and we give."

"Blame our damn mothers for teaching us that," said Tori.

"Blame the Patriarchy," said Carrie.

They toasted their drinks.

"Well, I think it won't hurt to wait a while before I talk to him," said Carrie. "He's taking Emily and Johnny to New Mexico for the Fourth, anyway."

"For how long?"

"Just a week. So I'm all yours, Tori. Let's plan a few nights out."

* * *

Carrie walked into the studio on a day free of classes. Emily was in New Mexico with Manny. Carrie planned to give all her time to her art this day. The art, she knew, would give her the ability to put everything into the right perspective, including how to fit Manny into her life. The art had all the right questions and all the right answers. It was just up to Carrie to put in the time, to create, until both the questions and the answers came.

First, she needed a layer of white gesso across the entire canvas. It was a large undertaking, tedious to some, but she treasured the time it allowed her to think.

Tori was right. Manny didn't always speak up; it was just his style to be laid back. But she was capable of speaking up. She could fight her own battles if she needed to. She never relied on him before, to do that. No sense in thinking she needed to do that now. That mindset that she needed any knight in shining armor was patriarchal nonsense.

What was this canvas going to become? A dream, the canvas answered. What dream? She heard Manny's voice saying, "you're in my dreams." Was that it, then? Could she paint herself in his dreams?

She put her brush down and shook her head. This was her canvas; she should pay attention to her own dreams.

Later that day, she was able to start with the colors. She trusted the process, letting it guide her. The dreams began to reveal themselves. The work was more realistic than her usual abstract style. It was layered, like her dreams. Her beautiful seashells and the mystical moon on the waters were meshed upon the canvas.

On the third layer, his eyes came. His beautiful eyes looked at her without judgment. They always made her feel like he knew her. Like he had always known her. They were different from each other in many ways, but when she looked into his eyes, she saw all the ways they were alike. She needed those eyes.

She drew the barest outline of his face and then detailed his hair. She stepped back to take it all in. There was the Sea, the beach, her daughter smiling, the moon and there, revealed for all to see, her lover, Mangus Chattoche. He was in her dreams; she must admit it to herself and the world. At some point, she realized, she must admit it to him.

She went to the supermarket to get some food. Near the register, a magnet caught her eye. "Life is Art. Paint your Dreams," it read. She smiled. That's exactly what she was doing.

The house felt empty after she ate. She was too tired to paint. She wandered the rooms.

There was a big, antique steamer trunk in her bedroom. She moved the plants that covered it and opened the trunk. It was lined with vintage wallpaper. Her mother had done that. Her father had cleaned the outside and cut an old leather belt, to create new strap handles. She had brought the trunk to College, full of her young dreams.

She breathed in the smell of years past. There were drawing books and journals, marble composition books and handmade cards, books of poetry and song lyrics. She could smell the patchouli candles she had once kept lit, through her long nights of writing and drawing. Turpentine was still strong, too, from several small canvases.

She opened a journal titled College.

So, my new life has begun. I started Art School today. I am so ready for this! My dreams will come true! Someday I'll be busy every day in my studio, painting for famous galleries. I will be so well known, and they will be happy to wait until I have something for them. I'll create a new technique – like Vincent did with his short lines of brush, like Seurat did with his points of paint, like Pollack did with his dripping from cans – I will be known for ???? Something! I will figure it out during the next few years here in school. The teachers that I've had so far, all seem super cool. I think I can learn a lot from them. There are about 10-15 kids that are in all the same classes as me. One guy, named Manny, is interesting. And cute! Really cute!

Carrie laughed. It was true. He was really cute back then.

She flipped through some pages, looking for his name.

A white envelope addressed to her childhood home, fell from the book. It was a letter from Manny, sent during Winter Break of freshman year.

*Dear Carrie,*

*I thought of you while I was drawing this. I hope you have a nice holiday with your family.*

*Happy New Year and see you soon,*

*Manny*

The drawing was a pen and ink of a mountain landscape. Why had he thought of her, when he was drawing mountains? Long, sensuous lines of the mountains contrasted with intricate details of clouds and shadows. Is this how he saw her? She realized, the longer she looked at it, just how much time it must have taken to draw. He was never afraid to give her all his time, no matter how long it took. Making art or making love, he always gave her as much time as she needed.

He had said Rachel didn't deserve an explanation of their relationship. He hadn't given Rachel any time. *Sometimes you walk away*, he had said to Emily. *Our people have already given enough. You don't owe an explanation.* She had heard him say that more than once. He didn't give his time, his energy, his words, his mood to just anyone that came along and demanded it.

She pulled out her phone and took a picture of his drawing, next to his note.

**I hope you're still thinking of me**, she texted to him and attached the image.

The reply came back immediately.

**Always.**

He attached an image of the same mountain view at sunset.

That surprised her. Considering the time difference, it was probably sunset where he was.

**Are you there now?** She texted.

**Yes. Looking at the mountains. Thinking of you. Praying for you.**

**Thank you**, she texted back. Tears came to her eyes. Even now, he was giving her his time, his energy, his prayers.

* * *

The next morning she walked along the beach. It never failed her. She felt the peace of nature. She walked on the dune trails, through scrubby pines and twisted oaks and holly bushes with their pointy, thorn-like leaves. The soft powder-blue berries in a sea of green needles on the fir trees inspired her with the contrast of their textures and colors. Life is beautiful, she thought, watching the sunlight filter through the canopy of the forest, hearing the surf pounding nearby, smelling sun on sand.

She could fight her own battles and let Manny choose to react how he wanted. She couldn't and wouldn't expect him to act like anyone but himself. She didn't want him to be anyone but himself. She needed Manny, the unique, the kind, and the sweet. Emily needed Manny, too. The world needed Manny, just the way he was.

Manny was...what was the word? She picked up a bright yellow feather nestled in a shell. He was different.

Different. He saw things differently than her and wouldn't waste his words or anger.

The water glittered on a pile of tiny pebbles. They glowed in the sun and looked precious. But she knew from experience, you take the same little pebble home and it just looks like a rock, when it's out of the sun, away from the sea. Some things don't translate well to another language, to another place.

She bent to the pebbles and flicked them, searching through the sand, for one tiny treasure. A rounded flash of ruby red sprang up, as her reward. Red beach-glass! The most precious, like fire. Like the fire inside when Manny loved her. She was going to have to apologize to him.

She put the bit of ruby glass and the yellow feather into her pocket. She would be nicer to him, starting today. She could, at the very least, be a friend to him.

Manny, in New Mexico, woke up to the sound of his father Joseph walking through the living room, where Manny was sleeping on the couch. The front door opened and he felt the coolness of the lingering night. He should get up and greet the dawn, too. He should walk in those footsteps now. His father wasn't going to wait for him.

He closed his eyes for only a second and the dream came back over him. All the women in his family surrounded him. No, there was more than his family. There were girls from his childhood, young women he had dated in high school. There was Donna, who was once happy to be his wife. Everyone was there, except Carrie. He shook his head, starting to wake again, trying to shake off the dream, when he saw the sheet of silver. It was covered with stamped designs, every inch used, to make a gift of jewelry for every woman there. Curious, he let himself sink back to the dream, to look at the designs. They were each geometric and each could be made with a tool he already had. Sometimes a design required him to create a new tool, but in the dream, he knew all these women would be happy with a gift made from what he already had.

But not Carrie. Carrie wasn't even in the dream. He had no design for her.

He opened his eyes and the sun was already bright through the curtains. It should have been a good dream. There was so much love. There were many smiles and even some kisses. But it left him with a feeling of being at a loss. He had nothing to give her.

The house was full of people, some just waking, some laughing and eating. He still didn't see his brother, Cochi, the traveling bluesman. He walked outside onto the porch and called him on the cell.

"Brother," said Cochi.

"Am I keeping you from your fans?"

"No fans in sight. They get hard to find outside New Mexico."

"Where are you?"

"That's a good question. I think this is California. No idea what town, though."

"I'm at Dad's for the Ceremony. I thought you'd be here. I brought Emmie and her friend Johnny."

"Good. I'll be there soon. Going to drive straight through after a gig tomorrow. What about Carrie, is she coming?"

"No. She doesn't want to talk to me right now."

Cochi had a good laugh. "Your big smile and your big muscles just weren't enough, huh? Now what are you going to do?"

"I don't know. Any ideas?"

Cochi laughed. "I can't believe I was feeling a little jealous of you, going off to be with your daughter, and pretty college sweetheart. Sounds like you're really screwing it up."

"I can always count on you to make me feel better."

"Well, what happened? I thought it was going good?"

Manny thought so too. "Carrie's like the ocean. She's calm one day and she's crashing waves the next. I'm okay with that, but sometimes she's not okay with me."

"Because you're just sitting there like a bump on a log in the sand?"

"Yeah, that's me," said Manny.

"Well, that's not going to change. That's the best thing about you, Bro. You're the steady rock, Man. You're the most Apache person I know - humble, compassionate, generous and steady - always walking the balance. Never letting anything ruffle your feathers. You know, sometimes women want an Alpha man to take over. You're no Alpha, dude."

"You've got a way with compliments."

"You're not going to be able to change, even if you want to," said Cochi.

"Mmm. I know you're right. I should just own it, who I am."

"Damn straight."

"Alright. I'll see you soon," said Manny. "Drive safe and pull over when you're tired."

Balance. Guzhuguja. This visit home would help him renew it. But it might mean he would become even less of what Carrie wanted. He was a sheet of silver, full of designs but none that interested Carrie. He was going to have to accept that.

Movement to his right caught his eye as he put his phone in his pocket. A woman alone, her back to him, was humming while dancing several yards away from the house.

Her shoulders high, her arms outstretched, a beautiful shawl swayed with her steps. He stared, transfixed. He felt so young, like watching his mother dancing. There was no time, there was only the fringe of the shawl swaying. She stopped. She looked back over her shoulder.

"Hi, Dad," said Emily, smiling.

He nodded, not sure he could speak. She twirled around, showing off the shawl.

"Isn't it beautiful? Auntie Sis gave it to me! She wants me to join her dancing tonight! I'm practicing."

He swallowed. "Beautiful. I remember when it was made."

"You do? Did you tell Auntie my colors? That I love purple and green?" She hugged the shawl to her body and walked up to him, her face turned up and lit by the sun.

"No. The woman that was my mother, she made it for you, Em."

"Oh." She looked down at the shawl, tracing the designs gently with her fingers. "But how did she know?"

"They were her colors, too," he said, just now remembering it.

"Oh! Cool!" Emily twirled again as the sun sparkled on her and she smiled to it.

Manny smiled, too.

* * *

Manny sat watching the Ceremony. He remembered what he saw, years ago, when he had gone to the Museum in New York City, of all places. The figures were clearly drawn on the small deer hide. Girls wrapped in blankets, walking in pairs. The Mountain God Dancers, the big fire, the Holy Lodge. It was all there. It had been experienced by the ancestors, the same as he was experiencing today. Same as he experienced every year. There had been a fading photograph of Naichi, the great leader of his people, the last leader of the free, next to the deer hide where Naichi had drawn the Ceremony. It was hard to see through the museum glass. He had an urge to punch the glass, to get a better look, to bring the hide back to the people where it belonged. But he stood silent and looked and his eyes adjusted to the glare on the glass. The hide was fading like the photograph. What was Naichi saying, when he drew the images? There was a truth, as long as the Ceremony went on, the people went on.

His daughter was his future, was the people's future. Trying to become a part of her life, he was trying to give her all he had, all he was from. He knew it fell far short of what could have been, but there was no way to go back. It was only now, and he was content that he had brought her to the ceremony this year and every year he had known her.

He took his eyes from the dancers and took a good look at Emily and Johnny, sitting in front of him. They were whispering to each other. Manny tapped them on the shoulders.

"Pay attention," he said. "This is important."

"What does it mean?" asked Johnny.

Manny frowned. "It's for you to find out what it means to you. You can't do that unless you pay attention."

At least they watched and listened then. And they laughed at the clown, along with the rest.

He felt good, hearing the laughter. His daughter was in front of him. His two brothers, Cochi and Little Bro, sat on either side of him. His father sat nearby. Aunties and cousins, and his two nieces surrounded him. This was his family.

His thoughts were wandering all over, but he let them. This, the time of Ceremony, was a time to listen to his thoughts.

Why had he moved to live near Emily and Carrie? He had been so determined, just a few months ago. Now nothing was going as he had thought it would. Again he thought of the hide and the photograph in the museum. Had anything gone the way Naichi had thought it would, spending decades in prison, being shuttled from place to place, across the nation? No.

Manny could find balance in a new environment. He had the same strength as Naichi and those who survived the genocide. His father had taught him. *It's not about where you live or what you wear. It's that you live. And it's about how you live.*

He could be a good father to Emily. He could be a good friend to Carrie, even if he wasn't her lover. He could go back to New Jersey and deal with all the obstacles and find a way to do it, without changing who he was, at his core. Without changing how he lived in this world. He would take the lesson from Naichi. He would live the circle of life.

* * *

On the flight back, Emily sat between Manny and Johnny. Manny was tired and closed his eyes. Emily and Johnny discussed everything they had seen, had done, had eaten and had felt the last week. He smiled, listening. He had been concerned they weren't paying attention, but they hadn't missed a thing. He could feel the bright sun coming through the clouds. He felt a bit homesick already, for the mountains he was leaving and so many of his family.

"Would you like a drink, sir?" asked the stewardess.

He opened his eyes to see a beautiful woman smiling at him.

"Just water, thanks."

"Are you going on vacation?" she asked as she poured.

"No," he said. "I'm going home."

It surprised him that he had said that. Home was now where Carrie and Emily lived.

"We were at the Girls Puberty Ceremony," said Emily.

"Is that the Apache ceremony?" asked the stewardess.

"Yeah, it was awesome," said Johnny. "Have you been to it?"

"No, I haven't, but I've heard about it. I'm Diné, from the Navaho Nation. We have our own ceremonies."

"My auntie is Diné," said Emily. "Oh. I wanted to ask you. Do you have any magazines that aren't so boring?"

"We do," said the stewardess, smiling. "Come back to my station after the meal and I'll show you a stack of them."

The stewardess smiled again at Manny.

When Emily went later to find her, Johnny talked to Manny. "So, your Dad, Emmie's grandpa, he's pretty cool," said Johnny.

Manny nodded. He waited, wondering what Johnny had liked about the old man.

"He's like, he's really into all the dancing and stuff, right?"

Manny nodded again. "He used to dance on the powwow circuit, went from state to state in the summer. He was good, got lots of prizes. I used to go with him sometimes when I was a kid."

"I wouldn't mind having a dad like that."

"Tell me about your dad, Johnny."

"I can't. I don't even know who he is. Definitely some loser."

"Maybe not. Even if he was, you know, people change," said Manny. "He could be anybody."

"He wouldn't care about me, anyway. Besides, it's too late."

"I don't know who your dad is or what he's like, but you know, I didn't know about Emily until she was ten years old. And when Carrie called me and told me about her, it was like my whole world changed that day, for the better. I've become a better person, since I've known about her, had her to live for. It put everything in my life into a new perspective. You might be surprised, in a good way, if you ever get to meet him, Johnny."

"Yeah, Emmie's pretty lucky. Really lucky. I wouldn't mind finding out my dad's Apache and getting to go to that festival every year."

"I'm glad you came."

"Nobody to stop me," said Johnny.

"Your foster mother didn't put up many questions about it when I asked for her permission."

"She don't care if I'm not there, as long as she gets paid for me."

"I got shuttled around a bit when I was young," said Manny. "It was always with relatives, though. And I had my two little brothers with me. I think that helped me get past feeling alone."

"I don't have any brothers or sisters. My Mom says I was a mistake."

"Where's your Mom?" asked Manny.

"I don't know," said Johnny. "Probably drunk somewhere or dead in a ditch, I don't know. I don't care."

Dead in a ditch. He hated that phrase. He put his hand on Johnny's shoulder. Was he steadying himself or comforting Johnny?

"It's okay to care," he said. "Caring is for the brave. I know you're brave, Johnny."

Johnny looked like he was holding back tears.

"My birthday's coming up," said Johnny, "in a month and a half."

"Okay, good. We'll celebrate it with you."

Johnny sniffed and nodded his head several times.

The Ceremony had a way of bringing emotions to the surface. It was best to deal with it in silence.

Emily came back with several magazines, looking triumphant. She slipped into her seat. "Dad, I had to tell the stewardess you're married to Mom."

"Why did you have to do that?"

"Because she was asking me too many questions about you. You really should do what I said and wear a ring."

Manny laughed. "I'm glad I have you here to watch out for me. But maybe instead of batting all the women away from me all the time, you could talk to your mother about what a great guy I am."

"Why?"

"She doesn't see it." He leaned back in the seat.

"I think you just misunderstood her, Dad."

"No misunderstanding it. Last time I saw her, uh, it was not so good of a goodbye. She doesn't see me like you do, Em. You know, we have different styles, your Mom and me."

"Well, I like your style, Daddy." She kissed him on the cheek.

"I like your style, too, Em," he said.

Emily and Johnny decided to watch a movie together, the same one on each of their individual screens.

"Are you gonna watch it, too, Dad?" asked Emily. "We can pause, so we all start together."

"No, not this one," he said.

A trailer for an upcoming horror film was showing on Emily's screen.

"Whoah, I've got to see that," said Emily to him.

"Me, too," he said. "We should ask your Mom to come with us. We saw the first one in that series together."

"Who?" Emily looked shocked or acted shocked. He could never tell. "My mom? Uh, Dad, this is awkward. I think you're mixed up with somebody else's mom."

He chuckled, but he didn't understand the joke. He and Carrie watched so many horror movies back in college.

"Very funny. I know who your Mom is."

"Yeah, the scarediest scaredy-cat alive."

He didn't remember Carrie ever being scared of anything. She was the one who sometimes dragged him to those films, wasn't she? Maybe she had decided Emily wasn't ready for them.

"Does she let you see horror films?"

"Of course. She's fine with me seeing most movies. She understands I need to be exposed to good acting. You know, since I'm an actress."

"Uh-huh."

The Missing Years. It wasn't only a young Emily he had missed out on. Carrie had gone through changes, too.

He closed his eyes while the kids watched the movie. No movies for him, he had his own story to dream.

Carrie opened the back door to the cottage after her morning walk and was surprised to see Emily opening the refrigerator.

"You're up early. I didn't expect to see you till noon, with the late flight in last night."

"I couldn't sleep. I keep thinking about all that happened."

There was something quiet about Emily today. She looked more reflective, not so dramatic.

Emily pulled out a carton of eggs. "I got to spend more time with Grandpa."

"That's nice."

"Alone time. I helped him do grocery shopping. I never realized how funny he is. He told me some stories about Dad."

Carrie raised her eyebrows.

"I'm not going to tell you, Mom! That's just between me and Grandpa. I think he was, you know, trying to let me know more about Dad. Anyway, I think Grandpa and Dad are a lot alike. Well, except, of course, Grandpa would never hug me, like Dad hugs me. Grandpa doesn't do that. But Grandpa taking me with him and telling me stories, it felt like a hug."

"That's what family feels like," said Carrie. Once, a long time ago, she knew that feeling.

"I wish I had a chance to meet your Dad," said Emily. She centered the frying pan on the burner. "Before he died, did he know, at least, that I was on the way?"

Carrie blinked. Emily had a way of catching her off guard. She wanted to tell her yes immediately. But she had promised herself no more white lies for Emily.

"I wasn't that far along. I didn't get a chance to tell him. But now that I think about it, I think he knew. Last time I saw him, the day before his heart attack, he told me, out of the blue, he said he loved me. I think he knew, Em."

That was the truth and now it was a gift that Emily gave her. She had never allowed herself to wonder about it before. Yes, of course he knew.

Emily smiled and cracked an egg on the side of the pan.

"Cool! That's really nice to know, Mom." She cracked another egg. "I got to know more about my grandma, Dad's mom, this week, too. And I got to dance for hours and hours in a beautiful shawl she made!"

"That sounds exhausting."

"It is, but. Well, I don't know how to explain how it felt. Dad says that's because it's Ceremony."

"I'm sure he's right, then. Did he have a good time too?"

Emily frowned. "He told me there's some problem between you two. I am not the go-between! You should ask him yourself if you want to know how he is."

When did Emily get so wise?

"You're right. I shouldn't ask you to be a go-between,

Em. I was so mad at him, but now I think I've been too hard."

"What did he do?"

"More like what he didn't do. He didn't stand up for me when Rachel Turner accused me of spray painting her car."

Emily froze. Her eyes went wide. "What?"

"Rachel Turner is telling everybody I spray painted her car. I think she probably did it herself, to set me up."

Emily still stood frozen.

Carrie turned the burner off and moved the frying pan from the heat, so Emily didn't burn the eggs. "Did someone besides Rachel do it, Emmie?"

Emily swallowed.

"Emmie, do you know who?"

Emily nodded her head yes as tears spilled down her cheeks. "I didn't think it would make you and Dad break up," she cried. "I'm so sorry."

"You did it? I can't believe it!"

"Johnny did it."

"That damn Johnny!"

"No, it's not his fault, Mom. I told him I wished someone would do it. I just wanted to get that lady away from Dad. I didn't know it would make you break up with him." Emily's face was full of tears now. "I'm sorry, Mom. I'm so sorry. I ruined everything!"

Carrie hugged her. "I think we need to tell your Dad."

Emily shook her head. "He already knows."

"You told him, but not me?"

"No, he figured it out right away. He went right to Johnny to talk about it. Then he had a long talk with me."

Carrie sighed. This was more complicated than she had thought. And Manny deserved more of her respect.

* * *

Carrie called Manny in the afternoon, giving him time to recoup from the trip home. His voice was sleepy.

"I woke you up."

"I shouldn't be sleeping anyway."

"Did you have a good time? I heard there was all night dancing involved."

"It was good. You should have seen Emily. She makes me so proud. You've done a good job raising her. Everybody says that. I want you to know that, Carrie."

"Aw, I'm glad she makes you proud. I think you have a lot to do with that. And how did Johnny do? Did he make you proud?"

Manny laughed. "He's alright. He just needs a break. Did you know he's been in the foster system for half his life?"

"No, I didn't know that. You know a lot more about him than I do. Speaking of that, I owe you an apology. Emmie told me about the spray paint this morning. You didn't want Rachel to figure it out and blame the kids, did you?"

There was a pause.

"I wasn't trying to throw you under the bus, Carrie."

He paused again, and she waited, knowing he had more to say.

"Rachel was demanding that I tell her about you and me. I wouldn't do that. You're too special; you're off-limits to her. Listen, I've been thinking a lot while I've been away. The Ceremony helped me see some things more clearly. Things have been out of order here. Wild. Crazy. It's my fault. I haven't worked hard enough to keep the balance."

"What balance?"

"Harmony. Beauty. We call it guzhuguja."

Carrie sighed. She knew his heart was in the right place, that he was a good man. Maybe the same way she didn't understand what he said sometimes, maybe she misunderstood things too.

"Let's try this again, Manny. Try us again? There's a place I want to show you today."

* * *

Manny stood at his opened door, watching her as she climbed the steps. She could feel the aching magnetism again, that pulled them to each other. With every step closer, she felt it stronger. Would he kiss her, now, after the way she'd left him last time she was here? She was afraid he wouldn't. But when she stepped onto the landing where he stood, they both reached to each other and sought each other's lips. He moved slightly and kissed the side of her face, into her hair. She loved the way he did that.

"I have plans for us today," she said.

He leaned back.

"Tell me your plans," he said, with his most charming smile.

She swore he knew how to make himself look irresistible. She was so tempted to ditch her plans for more of his kisses.

"I want to show you things today," she said. "I'm taking you to the boardwalk for a bit of Jersey Shore culture. And I'm treating you to dinner in an amazing seafood restaurant."

"This is because..?"

"This is because you deserve it. You've been patient with me. I am learning to trust you, that your ways can get to the same results as mine. Anyway, let's have fun today, okay?"

"I'm up for fun," he said as they left the apartment.

"Do you remember Asbury Park? That's where I'm taking you."

"Sure. I remember going down there to the clubs, after the restaurant closed, with the kitchen crew. We heard some good music there."

"Yeah, it's still a great music town. But there's much more to it, now. It's going through a renaissance. There's a community of artists, musicians, great little independent restaurants, galleries. I love it. Plus, it has the boardwalk and the ocean, of course. Everything that's needed."

"No mountains?" he asked.

"I'll show you my mountains. Get in the car."

* * *

She parked near the beach. They walked on the sand and then sat on a bench that allowed them to watch the crowds walking the boardwalk, with the ocean to their back.

"I love people-watching the most," she said. "This place is so Jersey. I love how there are people from all classes and all cultures, here together to enjoy the ocean and the cool breeze."

"I've heard more languages spoken here than at an Intertribal Powwow."

"Well, you're probably the only one who speaks Apache."

"That might not be true. It doesn't matter, anyway. I know English."

"And words aren't worth much to you, right?"

She said it flippantly, making a joke. He looked at her.

"They're not enough," he said.

She nodded. Okay, she should rethink this. She wasn't here to make chitchat all day. She wanted to give him something. Maybe it was a vision of what she thought of as her culture? The good side of it? What she was proud of? And why did she want to do that? Was she afraid he would decide to go back to New Mexico? How could she hope to compete with all that it offered him?

Later, they sat at a table for two at a boardwalk restaurant. The cool, salt air had a refreshing breeze.

"How is the job going?" she asked. "What does the new semester look like?"

He shrugged.

"Long hours and not at all what I thought I'd be doing. They're putting me out on the Hook starting Monday. There won't be much teaching."

"What will you be doing?"

"I'm not sure of the details yet. I don't want to talk about that today. Whatever I have to deal with at work, I can deal with it on Monday."

Talk of work was off-limits? Is that how he intended to keep the balance? Rachel or Tom Turner must be involved in the work. She let it pass, with some effort. It was his job. He could deal with whatever manipulations of him that Rachel and her father might try. She had to trust he could.

After eating, they walked to the gallery where some of Carrie's paintings had just been hung. The gallery was a perfect match for Carrie's art, to be so near the ocean.

"I love your paintings," said Manny. "You capture the Sea so well."

"It's a part of me," said Carrie. "That makes it easy to do."

"It's definitely a part of you. I can't even look at the ocean without thinking of you."

"Have you seen it during a storm?"

"I've seen you storming into my apartment. I have an idea what it's like to be inside a hurricane."

She laughed. If he wasn't afraid of her raging storms, then he was stronger than most men she'd met.

They walked through a skeleton of a building. The decaying wood facade still said CASINO. Beyond it was more boardwalk.

"Now we're in Ocean Grove," she said, "a very peculiar little place. It's still officially a Methodist campground. Most of the buildings were put up at the same time and replaced tents."

"Amazing examples of Victorian Gingerbread," he said.

They walked the Main Street of Ocean Grove, then cut back through a maze of little streets to a footbridge over a lake that led back into Asbury Park. A large sign on a pair of black iron gates warned, 'Gates Locked at Midnight.'

"Are these for real?" asked Manny.

"Yes! I told you it's a peculiar place! I'm not sure if it's to lock the artists out or the innocents in."

They quickly crossed to the Asbury Park side of the gates and walked up Cookman Ave as she pointed out renovated buildings. There was a row of galleries, restaurants, and unique artisan shops. Several artists she knew, greeted her as they walked.

They passed a movie house. The marquee showed the new horror movie was coming soon.

"That's a movie we should see," he said.

"You and Em, maybe. I'll pass on that one."

"Why? You used to drag me to everything made by that director."

"Really? I don't remember that." She kept walking.

"You did. What happened?"

She turned to look at him. "What happened? I grew up. I had a baby. That's what happened!"

They kept walking.

"Okay," he said after a few moments.

"No, not okay. You don't get it." She looked around for what? For words? "Look, I'm not a naive little college girl anymore. I don't have to wonder what it's like to be scared. I'm all grown up. And I learned being scared is not my idea of fun."

She stopped. Stop with the words. Words say too much.

"No problem," he said. "When we're together, you pick the movies."

She smiled. "Chick Flicks? Then what do you get out of it?"

"Kisses and popcorn?"

"Ha. You're always looking at the end result, aren't you, Manny?"

The darkness of a moving cloud was gone. The sun was all bright and teasing.

"That's right. I don't care how we get there," he said.

"We don't even need a movie, then, if you time it right."

They were passing an alley and she pulled him into it, laughing, her face close to his.

"But popcorn. I like popcorn," he whispered.

"I'll pop your corn," she said.

They both giggled as they took a minute to kiss.

She felt hot. It was a hot day and they had walked for hours, not to mention the inner heat growing.

"Let's get a drink," she said. She led him to a nearby rooftop bar.

"This town suits you," said Manny, when the drinks

came. "You know everybody here. The ocean is here. There are places that support your art. I think you belong here."

"Did Emily tell you?"

"Emily never mentioned Asbury Park."

Carrie laughed. "I guess it's just another example of you knowing what I want, Manny. You're right about this town," she said, after sipping a rum punch. "This is where I belong. I'm always telling Emily, I'm going to move here when she goes off to college. I love it on the Hook, but as an artist, I need to keep changing. This town has a good community of artists. I'd like to join it someday."

"Change is good. Strength comes from change. College isn't far off. She's going into Junior year."

"I know. We're going to have to start dealing with helping her choose a college."

Carrie left unsaid that meant talking about tuition. That was a discussion for another day.

Manny looked out at the rooftop view of the lake that separated Ocean Grove and Asbury Park. Carrie followed his gaze. There was a large Swan pedal boat on the water.

"This town is an interesting mix of architectural styles," said Manny. "I need to arrange some field trips here with my classes."

He looked at some new construction nearby. "Looks like there's still some rebuilding going on."

"There's plenty of rebuilding going on," said Carrie. "It's still possible to buy a big old house here and renovate it for a reasonable amount."

"Is that what you want to do?" he asked. His eyes looked into hers with that way he had of seeing her, really seeing her.

"That's what I'd love to do. I'd make the first floor a gallery and studio - the second floor for living space. Then a floor of bedrooms. All with an ocean view, of course. That's my dream."

"You might need an architect to help with that dream."

"True. I'll have to find one somewhere. And money, lots of money."

He put his hand over hers.

She felt warm. She questioned herself. Why had she wanted him to come here and walk the streets with her, visit the art galleries, and taste the food? Was it because she wanted him to live here with her so they could find new adventures together? She pushed the thought away. She was just having fun with him, sharing a place that made her happy.

* * *

It was getting late when they got back to Manny's apartment. He clicked his playlist on, and the speakers filled the room with music. He pulled her gently to the couch. His eyes were sleepy, heavy-lidded, and he seemed to have nothing else on his mind, but kissing her. How could a man be so good at kissing?

"You are the best kisser ever, Manny. Do you know that?"

"I know that," he murmured, kissing her again.

His kisses were truly sweet, making her feel treasured and loved.

She laid her back on the couch.

He leaned over her.

"You look like you want me to touch you," he whispered.

"You're right. I'm waiting for you to touch me."

"What about looking? Can I look at you?"

She hesitated to say yes. Strange, she felt more nervous about him looking at her than touching her.

His eyes were waiting. She nodded slightly and he replied with a slight gleam in his eyes and a touch of a smile. She watched him look her over slowly. He may as well be touching her. She was burning even more with each moment his stare lingered.

She was determined not to squirm. She willed herself to let him go ahead. His eyes lowered and then he looked up, back to hers. His stare on her felt hotter than his hands could be.

She looked him over in return, allowing herself to study those tight jeans, that belt buckle, that lovely bulge that she suddenly wanted to touch, to rub, to feel.

She looked up to see him with just a touch of a smile. His eyes were locked into hers.

It felt like making love without touching. How did he know how to do this?

"Have you done this with all your girlfriends?"

"I can't think of any woman but you right now."

She could tell him, 'you always know the right thing to say,' but she had no will to speak. She had no will to do anything except feel her body grow hotter beneath his gaze. Would he ever touch her?

He was looking at her breasts now. She couldn't stand it.

"Take my dress off." It was more of a plea than a command.

"I'm not done looking."

"You're cruel."

"I'm not cruel. I'm just slowing down, like you said we should."

"Did I say that? What was I thinking?" she sighed. But he was right. She sat back up next to him.

"I like that you picked me up today and showed me where you want to live," he said.

She suddenly felt shy about it. "I don't know why I felt it was so important to show you that today."

"I know why. You trusted me today with your dreams. That means a lot."

He was right. Again.

"We're making progress," she said. It made her feel stronger.

Carrie pulled up to the cottage and saw Emily and Johnny on the porch. Johnny was always around now.

"Hi, kids," she said. "Did you guys make yourselves dinner?"

They nodded.

"I had a couple of dinners," admitted Johnny.

Carrie laughed. "That's okay. That's good. I buy too much food, anyway."

"So...Mom," said Emily. "Tell us, what did you and Dad do today?"

Emily looked at Johnny. They both smirked.

"We had a beautiful day, *walking* around Asbury Park."

Emily laughed. "So, you guys are getting along now?"

"Yeah, we're getting along."

"Why doesn't he live here?" asked Johnny.

Emily hit Johnny's leg. "Johnny!" she said.

"What? I mean, he's your dad, right? You guys are a family."

Carrie smiled at Johnny. "It does seem silly, doesn't it, Johnny? I'm starting to wonder the same thing."

Manny woke up early to greet the sun as it rose from the ocean. Today, he would need whatever blessings he could find. It was his first day to go to work for Thomas Turner. It was a day to confront Rachel, to find out exactly why he'd been hired and why she'd been following him. But confrontation went against everything inside him.

There was no balance in confrontation. It was like a knot in his stomach. The Elders he respected the most rarely even asked a direct question. Always allow others to choose to give information or not. If a person was uncomfortable or embarrassed with your words, the embarrassment was on you, not them. Had Rachel taken advantage of that? She knew him well enough to know he'd rather not confront her.

Rachel was already at the office when he arrived. She seemed embarrassed to see him. Instinctively, he gave her a warm smile to make her feel comfortable.

"Good morning," he said.

"Hello." Her voice sounded small. "My father's not in yet."

Why did she always mention her father? Did she think people only thought of her as an extension of her father?

She was wearing a suit that was so well tailored he wondered if he was underdressed. He hadn't even brought a suit jacket.

"There's coffee in the break room over here, if you want," she said, walking towards the other side of the room.

He entered the small kitchen. It was a tiny room. She stood in the doorway and looked at him. She was a beautiful woman, somewhere, under all the makeup and polish.

He poured a cup and took a sip.

"I'm sorry about what happened to your car," he said. "I hope you know. I had no part in that. You've always been kind to me. I wouldn't do that to you."

She shifted her weight on her heels.

"You didn't do anything wrong," she said. "It was Carrie."

"That's not true."

"Manny, listen, I understand her jealousy. Believe me, it's not new to me. I get it from women all the time, especially women like Carrie. I'm successful, I dress well. Let's face it, I'm wealthy. I've got everything they don't have. I'd probably feel envious too, if I were in their shoes."

He opened his mouth to laugh but quickly put the mug to his lips to hide it. She was so far off the mark on Carrie. But that in itself was revealing. Maybe Carrie had everything Rachel didn't have?

What did Carrie have? Creativity? A voice of her own? A daughter? A best friend? Love? Everything Rachel didn't have.

She turned around and walked back to her desk. He followed her.

"Listen, it's going to be odd working together, for both of us," she said, as she sat down. "We need to clear the air."

"That's what I'm trying to do," he said. "Can you tell me what's really going on here, Rachel?" He pushed himself to get specific. "Why tell me about the job? Why show up when I was with my daughter at the restaurants and stores, and then the art show, when I was first here, as if you were following me?"

She looked out the window, anywhere but at him. He felt as uncomfortable as she looked. He was failing at this.

"I was attracted to you," she mumbled.

"That's not it," he said gently. "I know it's not. We go back a long time. You're friendly, but you don't flirt with me. I know when a woman's flirting with me."

Maybe it was strange she didn't flirt with him. But so many women did that he had always appreciated it from her. She had always been nothing more than a friend, always offering to help however she could. He never felt he had anything she wanted in return. Until, maybe, now.

"Rachel, if you tell me, maybe I can work with you to give you what you need."

She looked at him then, surprise and maybe hope on her face.

"You're a unique man, Manny. You always surprise me. It's simple. My father asked me to keep an eye on you, to socialize with you, because you're important to us, to the success of this project. And this project is very important to us.

"What can I say? I thought we were friends. I didn't think you'd mind. I do a lot of things for my father. You know, he's a very successful man. He's won so many awards, we've lost count. But he can't do everything on his own. He is needed so much in the business community. There's so much to do. I'm what you would call the woman behind the man. He needs me and I can't let him down. I'm sure you can understand.

"As far as why you're here - well, we knew when we suggested your position to the University that we needed whoever filled it to come work with us. We need someone with your expertise to get state approval on the project. I told you about the University position because I thought it was a win-win. We needed you and I knew you'd like to be near Emily. And I'm sure Emily wants to live near you. My mother kept me away from my father when I was young. I know what it's like. I'm sorry Emily is living in one of the buildings we need to tear down. I didn't know about that when I told you to apply. It's purely a coincidence."

"I don't believe in coincidence," said Manny.

"Maybe you can think of it as an opportunity then. If Carrie loses her home, I'm sure it would help you to gain full custody of Emily, right?"

"What? I would never..."

"It's okay, Manny. You don't have to admit it. I know you wouldn't hurt a fly and you like to let things just pass over you. As a friend, I'm just trying to do the heavy lifting for you. I know it's not the way you want to do it, but if you get what you want in the end, does it really matter? And also, if you haven't realized it, the police report on the spray painting of my car can't do anything but help your case."

*What the hell, Rachel?*

A car pulled up into the parking space near the window. Tom Turner got out.

"Rachel, you've got it all wrong."

"Shh. Please. Let's not talk about this in front of my father. He hates to get into messy details."

When Tom Turner entered Manny expected a confrontation, but there was none. He acted gracious and happy that Manny was now on his team.

"I met you at the meeting," said Manny, thinking maybe the man didn't realize who he was.

"I know. I was happy to find out who you were. Happy to have you onboard," said Turner, shaking his hand. "Here, come into my office for a minute. Make yourself comfortable."

Turner hung his suit jacket on a hanger behind the door, while Manny sat in a chair opposite his desk. The room had the smell of new paint. Everything looked perfectly new. It was decorated like an Executive Suite in a hotel. The artwork matched the carpet and obviously, the carpet was purchased first. No one would buy that painting for any other reason.

So Turner had money, but no taste. Interesting.

The other walls were covered in well framed award documents and photographs of Turner either giving out gigantic checks or receiving a trophy. Funny, there was one where the same man receiving a check was in the next photo giving back a trophy. *This project is very important to us. It's a win-win.* How big of a trophy was this project worth?

"This is our first week in the office here," said Turner, sitting behind his large desk. He looked at the walls, smiling.

"As you can see, I'm a busy man. I have quite a bit on my plate right now. But enough about me, tell me about yourself, Manny!"

*How to influence people. Rule 1. Let the other person do*

*most of the talking. Listen actively. It will make him trust you.*

There was a flash of discomfort on Turner's face. A moment of silence. Silence was so uncomfortable to some people.

"Emmanuel? Is that your full name? Or the Spanish Manuel?"

*Rule 2. Speak the person's name. There is nothing sweeter to anyone but to hear their name.*

"No," said Manny. He didn't need anyone speaking his full name, certainly not Tom Turner, to know it was special.

"I see you've got that brand of boots, there, said Turner quickly. "Best brand there is, custom handmade. I can tell you've been through Santa Fe. I've got a pair myself. Best boots on the planet. Not wearing them today, though."

Switch to the salesman's playbook.

*Rule 1. Find something about the customer to compliment.*

Turner moved his hand slightly in the air, gesturing at the boots.

*Don't wave your hand at me, Jedi. I'm a Toydarian. Mind tricks don't work on me.*

Stop.

He should stop being cynical and throw the guy a bone.

"They are the best boots," said Manny. "You're the first person in New Jersey to notice."

*Win-win!* Turner looked proud of himself. He'd cracked the case. He reached across to shake Manny's hand again.

"Good to meet you, Manny. Rachel will be able to fill you in on details about the project, now."

Rachel did fill him in. He was relieved to discover, the work itself would be interesting, at least. There were over a hundred structures on the Hook, built from the 1600s to the

1950s, most by the US Army. Each needed analysis of their history, an inspection of the current state, and a proposal with blueprints for future use or demolition. His days would be a mix of office work and exploring the Hook. He would drive by Carrie and Emily's house on his way to and from work. He'd be just a few minutes away from them all day. It would be easier now to have Emily spend the night at his place and be back at Carrie's in the morning. That was all positive.

On the other hand, it looked like there would be pressure for him to interpret the analysis and proposals to benefit Turner and his business associates. Rachel clearly assumed he'd go along with whatever they wanted. There was already a meeting scheduled with a group of CEOs who had their own ideas of the future use of specific buildings.

He skipped lunch and took a walk on the Old Dune trail instead.

Was he too compassionate? Was he gullible? Maybe he had been, with Rachel. Maybe all along her help to him had been transactional. It was hard to believe. He had never noticed. Still, no matter how misguided she was, he didn't understand her relationship with her father. What other kind of things did she do for her father? What other things did he ask of her? Manny didn't even want to know.

One thing he knew, for sure. He needed to keep quiet about this to Carrie, at least until he could figure a way out of it.

Working on the Hook allowed Manny to spend his lunch hours with Carrie, although she often used that time to paint in her studio. Manny didn't mind. He loved watching her paint. He pretended to be reading, but his book could have been upside down. She moved so much while she painted, almost like she was dancing with the canvas. She paused.

"My lover is clothed in white canvas. With him, I dance to find the music of my brush," said Manny.

Carrie laughed. "Oh my god! I wrote that a lifetime ago. You remembered! I can't believe it."

"I'd love to read the poetry you're writing these days."

"Writing? I don't write anymore. Haven't you noticed? I paint," said Carrie, looking back at her canvas.

"So, the painting won, totally?"

"Hmm?"

"That battle. You were always torn between the two. You didn't want to give either one up. How did you decide?" asked Manny.

"I don't remember making a decision." She shook her head. "All I know is that I hate writing now."

"Hate? That's a strong word."

"Yup, hate. Words are so, so, naked! They just sit out there waiting for someone to read them. They don't have any mystery."

"Mystery?" She was a mystery. He looked around the space at her recent paintings. All abstracts. An abstract was a mystery or a puzzle. "You don't paint portraits anymore, do you?"

"I still paint portraits."

"Oh, I see one over there, a mermaid."

"And I'm working on one of Tori."

"Another mermaid?"

She shrugged and smiled in agreement. She looked around the room, searching for something. She looked annoyed. He should drop it. She had found her voice. He was just curious how she had gotten there.

She moved some canvasses so he could see more work. "It's not all abstracts, see. I put sea creatures in my collages and the underwater seascapes."

Yes, she did. But it struck him that the water was like a veil, a filter, a distance that cloaked the view. And what did she show you in that glimpse you managed to see through the seaweed and bubbles? A fantasy world. He looked back at one of the abstracts. There was so much in it. The colors, the textures, the movement. It was almost overwhelming in chaos. And yet, it all worked together. If felt right. It would be hard to put into words, true.

*Words are so naked.* That was an odd thing to say. Words made her feel naked? And so paintings made her feel clothed? Cloaked? Hidden? Mysterious. Unknown.

That was Carrie's voice. No bullshit, yet you'll never know her.

She was watching him, unsure of something.

"I love it all," he said.

She smiled. "It's nice to talk about art with you, Manny. That's one thing I can't talk to Tori about."

"You have artist friends."

"Mmm. But I don't know why, I'm not close enough with them to share much besides techniques."

She needed him? Is that what she was saying?

"I'm here, whenever you want to share anything," he said.

"I know," she said, turning her back to him, with a brush in her hand, she streaked a scarlet line across a milk white space.

She said it as though it wasn't a big deal. Like she counted on him, to be here. He wanted to pick her up and twirl her around the room.

"That's a brave red line," he said, walking up to her.

"Mmm, I love this contrast, like a cardinal in the snow," she said, still looking at her canvas.

He put his hands on her shoulders and she screamed.

"It's me," he said as she spun around.

"What are you doing, Manny?"

"Nothing. I didn't mean to scare you."

"I'm not scared." She laughed, but it sounded forced. "I know it's you."

"Emmie told me you're an easy scare. I didn't realize ..."

"I'm jumpy. Yeah, Emily makes fun of me. It's automatic. I jump or scream when I'm surprised."

"Is that something to see a doctor about?"

"Why? I'm jumpy, that's all. Lots of people scare easily. It doesn't bother me. Does it bother you?"

"Of course not. I don't want you to be scared of me, that's all."

"Just stay where I can see you, then."

When had she told him that before? How many times had he scared her?

He opened his arms. "Okay. I just wanted to hug you."

She put her brush down and slid into his embrace. He closed his eyes, holding her. He wanted to hold her forever.

After a moment, she slowly withdrew and looked up at him.

"Thanks," she said, smiling. "I needed that."

"Any time," he said.

* * *

Gum popped. The artificial grape scent filled the room. Manny smiled.

Emily moved from the doorway and came into the kitchen, where he had set up a makeshift tool bench. He liked it when she watched him work on the metal.

"Who did you learn this from?" She snapped the gum.

"Your grandmother."

"Grandma Shannon?"

"No, Shannon is Grandpa's second wife. The woman that was my mother, she taught me."

"Oh, cool! Nobody ever talks about her. I think it's cool she was a metalsmith."

"Sit here and watch me," he said. "That's how I learned from her."

She sat on a stool next to him. He leaned and kissed her forehead.

"A daughter is special," he said. "In my family, there were no daughters, only three sons."

"And you were the oldest!"

He waited to reply while he lined up the tool and then hammered it.

"Mmm, I was the oldest. So, I had to watch the others."

"Why? Where were your parents?"

She snapped the gum again and again.

He hesitated. He hadn't meant to go into that.

"My father was gone working most of the week."

"And what about your Mom?"

He remembered being Emily's age. His Mom had been home for several months. They were working side by side, making silver combs. His mother looked at him, and he could see she was proud. He was happy to help her, with the metal and with his brothers. That day, it had felt like, maybe, she would stay around forever.

She popped a bubble.

"We don't talk about the dead," he said.

Emily frowned and stopped chewing.

He felt her disappointment. He would somehow share more with her someday. For now, this was the only way he knew.

"I think I should make something for your Mom. I never made her any jewelry."

"She likes earrings."

He looked at Emily's earrings - long silver hoops. Her long black hair, just like his, was pulled back tight. Carrie's clear blue eyes stared at him.

"Are those her earrings?"

"Yeah. These are too thin for her. She won't miss them."

"Okay. She likes earrings. Not a ring?"

"She doesn't like rings, because her hands are always covered in paint. She said wedding rings are not worth the hassle. She doesn't ever want to wear another ring, especially a wedding ring."

Manny laughed. Then he laughed a little more.

"Alright. It has to be earrings. Big earrings."

"Huge earrings! She hates tiny earrings. She says she's got big hair, so she needs big earrings and she doesn't need those tiny, timid earrings everybody else wears these days."

"We won't be timid, then. We'll design something big and bold, like her."

"And loud. She's loud."

"Truth."

The gum popped.

He reached for his sketchbook. He sketched large domed ovals.

"And you need a design for the beach. That's her favorite place."

"I'm ahead of you on that." He was already drawing ripples of waves. "I'll have to make a new tool to get it just right for her."

"What metal are you going to use?"

"Copper. It has to be copper for her."

"Why?"

He smiled. "Copper is like a woman."

He stopped. Better not explain how the touch of hammer on copper reminded him of Carrie. She'd move to accommodate him, she was warm and receptive, but she kept her cool, crisp edge. Copper would do whatever you needed and still keep its own style, still make you realize, in the end, that maybe it was her idea all along.

The gum popped.

"How the hell is copper like a woman, Dad?"

"Warm. Soft. Yet it holds its own. It's my favorite metal to work in."

"What about silver? Or gold?"

"Silver's pretty, but it's finicky. And it won't listen or take you where you want to go. It pushes back. You have to anneal it too much, take care of it. It won't do anything on its own."

"That sounds more like a woman."

He laughed. He suddenly remembered the dream he'd had before the Ceremony, with the sheet of silver designs when all the women in his life appeared. There was something for all of them in silver, all of them except Carrie.

"Mmm. Some women. Most women. Not your Mom."

"And gold?"

"Gold is good. Gold is like a partner, especially a high karat gold. It goes along with you, nice and easy."

"That doesn't sound like Mom."

"Maybe someday she'll be nice and easy with me. Then I'll make her something in gold."

Emily watched him as he sketched several variations of the earrings.

"I like this design the best," she said, pointing to the first of the four designs he'd made. There was something familiar about the shape of it.

It was later when Em had gone back to texting her friends. The radio was playing obscure vinyl punk. He sawed to the drum beats. He remembered. Mom's favorite pair. She'd been loud and bold too.

He stopped sawing.

He wished she could have met Carrie and Emily. He wished they could have met her.

He started sawing again.

Earrings for Carrie, big and bold, like her heart. He prayed deep into the copper he sawed, let her know, I embrace her, I love her. Forever.

E mily had Carrie and Manny's full attention as they sat at the kitchen table. She waved her arms and sighed loudly.

"I *have* to go to this music festival," she said again. "This could be the most important event in my life. It's like Woodstock! Would you have chosen to miss Woodstock if you were alive then? How lame would that be?"

"What year was Woodstock?" asked Manny.

"It's not Woodstock!" said Carrie. "This festival is an annual event. And I don't think I'd let my daughter go to Woodstock, anyway."

Her mother wouldn't have let her go, but she'd have gone anyway. She wouldn't have even asked her mother. She couldn't tell Emily that.

"Oh, wait. I think Cochi usually plays this festival," said Manny.

"Uncle Cochi! He can tell you it's okay! He can watch me. You've got to let me go!"

Carrie caught Manny's eye. He was ready to give in, she could tell. Emily had him wrapped around her finger.

"So, the plan is Johnny's driving the four of you to North Carolina on Friday? You'll camp at the festival for two nights and be back Sunday night?" said Carrie.

Emily nodded, but her eyes were wide.

"What else?" said Carrie. Her Mom-detection knew there was more.

"Well, we might make a quick tiny side trip on Sunday to a little town nearby. Johnny thinks maybe he could find his mom there. But we'll drive straight back after that and still be home by Monday morning."

Carrie started to shake her head, no.

Manny reached out and squeezed her hand like a signal to wait.

"Has he heard from his Mom recently?" he said.

"No, nobody has in years. But he remembers he had cousins in this town. He's hoping he can find them. Maybe they know where she is. Maybe she's even there with them."

It sounded like a wild goose chase to Carrie.

"The festival is one thing," said Carrie. "Four teenagers in a broken down car in a small country town knocking on doors sounds like a B-level horror movie just waiting to happen."

"I can look at his car. Make sure everything's okay with it." Manny was looking right at her as he spoke. "And I can get Cochi to take care of them at the festival."

Why was it so important for Manny to let Emily go?

"You don't even know if he's playing there," said Carrie.

"He IS. He IS," shouted Emily. She was texting furiously, looking at her phone.

"He said we could stay in his room at the hotel and get STAFF passes so we can eat free at the buffets! Oh my God, we're going to be eating with the stars! All we have to do is get there!"

This was happening too fast. An anxious feeling gripped Carrie. She looked at Manny.

"I'll take his car to the shop and get everything checked out," said Manny, calmly. "I'll buy him new tires if he needs them."

She looked at Emily. She saw herself in those eyes, that beautiful naive face. She wasn't sure how innocent Emily was anymore. She would have to have a good talk with her soon to find out. At least she was on birth control.

Carrie stood up and walked to the window, looking out to the grasses swaying in the breeze on the dunes.

The gripping anxiety was taking over. She could think of everything that could possibly go wrong. How much of that was from her own past and bad choices? How much was she projecting? Emily was different than her. Manny was here, planning how it could go right. Who wouldn't want to go to Woodstock if they could?

"Maamumm," Emily pleaded.

"It's on you, Manny," Carrie said. "If anything happens."

"YASSS!" Emily jumped up and hugged Carrie. "Thank you! Thank you! Thank you, Mommy! I love you!" She kissed Carrie and ran to hug Manny. "Thank you, Daddy! You're the best dad ever!"

Carrie and Manny laughed as Emily ran out the door to tell Johnny and the others.

"She'll be alright," said Manny. "I'll tell Cochi. I'll kill him if anything happens."

"I'll wait for you to do that before I kill you," said Carrie.

Manny nodded with a serious look. Then his sexy smile spread over his face.

"We get a whole weekend alone."

"That's the first thing I thought about. We are terrible parents."

* * *

Emily would be gone three nights. Three long nights that Carrie and Manny could have together, without worrying about what doors were closed, or how much noise they were making. Three long nights, plus two long weekend days of being able to talk freely. They were both looking forward to it. That's what they told each other.

And that's what Carrie thought until Friday night came. She struggled to put on a cute dress and a little makeup before Manny came over. Sometimes, just getting ready to see a man was such a pain. Nothing was fitting right today. Her stomach was bloated and uncomfortable. Every bra jabbed into her. Her brain was aching from a headache.

It didn't take Manny long to notice.

"Something's bothering you, I can tell," he said, soon after he arrived.

"No. It's nothing."

She saw a flicker of frustration on his face.

"I'm good at listening," he said. His face was open and encouraging.

Men. He had no idea.

She smirked. "It's something, but it's nothing. It's just my time of the month. I'm feeling drained, literally. I just want to crawl into a hole and eat chocolate. It's nothing to do with you."

He looked relieved. "That's easy. I can deal with that."

He stood up and got an afghan from the chair. "First, we make you comfortable. Wrap you in blankets, get more pillows out here on the couch. Then what? I make you tea for when I go to the store and get chocolate?"

It was 80 degrees and humid. She didn't need a blanket, but she liked him tucking it around her.

"And ice cream. Get mint chocolate chip ice cream too."

"No problem. Anything else?"

She hesitated. She would hate to get mad at him tonight. "One thing."

"Yes?"

"My *own* carton of ice cream. If you're going to have some, get two."

He laughed. "No sharing?"

"Don't make me do that tonight."

He gave her a quick kiss. "You don't have to do a thing. Let me take care of you tonight, whatever you need, even if it's kicking me out so you can rest."

"I might do that. Or maybe we can binge watch some TV together?"

"Sounds good. Your choice."

* * *

While Manny was at the store, Carrie changed into her most comfortable jammies. She didn't even look in the mirror. If he could finish this night, as well as he started, she'd have to rethink her opinions about men in general and Manny in particular.

"I bought a few extra things," he said as he walked through the door.

"Flowers? Oh, they're so pretty, Manny. That's so sweet."

"And this, too," he said, handing her a book.

"A romance novel? By my favorite author?"

"Do you have this one yet?"

"No! But I've meant to get it. How do you know this?"

"Oh, good. I saw it says it was just released. I noticed you read her books. I've seen them around the house."

She stared at him. She had no words, no joke ready for this.

"My stepmom Shannon reads them too. I know they're a thing that makes some women happy."

She shook her head and took a good look at him. "Are you for real, Mangus Chattoche?"

He laughed. "I think I'm real. I feel real."

"I don't know," she said. "You're a little too perfect. It makes me wonder."

"Are you going to kick me out then?"

"No, I'm holding onto you tonight, keeping you in my sight. I need to make sure you don't shapeshift back into words in this romance novel."

"I'm no hero," he said, sitting down next to her on the couch. "I'm just a guy willing to buy you your own carton of ice cream and hand you the remote."

"Mmm. Well. You go on, thinking it's no big deal. I won't argue that it shouldn't be."

She ate a spoonful of ice cream and powered on the TV. He looked ahead at the screen, but she was reluctant to look away from him.

* * *

They spent most of a rainy Saturday working together in Carrie's studio. She painted as Manny sketched her. He went to the gym for a few hours while Carrie rested and read her new romance novel. Emily kept them, and the rest of the world updated on the festival through live streaming. Carrie could see exactly where she was. It was sunny weather there. In Jersey, the rain continued.

On Sunday, the rain was relentless. Manny cooked Carrie a big breakfast. She felt so pampered. She couldn't ever remember feeling truly pampered.

Tori texted her. They were both excited about the season finale of a dramatic show that would air this night. Carrie mentioned it to Manny.

"Why doesn't Tori come over so we can watch it together?" he said.

"She gives me space when you and I are together."

"You're right. She's never around when I'm around. That feels odd."

"It's not odd. It's respectful," said Carrie.

"But then, when do you get to see her? You and I are together almost every day or night now."

"Mmm..that's true."

Was she doing this again? Was she pushing Tori away because of a man in her life? What else was she pushing away? She was amazed it was Manny that noticed first.

"You don't mind if she comes over?"

Even as she said it, she knew it sounded wimpy, so unlike herself.

She didn't wait for an answer. She kissed him on the cheek.

"Okay, I'm telling her to come over. And you, by the way, are scoring massive points this weekend."

"I'm winning?"

"You're winning. This better not be a freaking act. Remember - this is your standard."

"Wait. What have I done?" He looked genuinely confused.

"Just stay as sweet as you are, Manny. And don't break my heart. That's all you need to remember."

"Got it," he said and smiled that sexy smile.

Tori came with goodies. She had grocery bags hanging from both arms. She clutched a big thick book to her chest.

"What did you bring?" said Carrie, looking at it.

"I brought fun! I brought snacks! I brought wine!" Tori said.

Carrie pointed and her inner-mom voice growled. "No, what is *that*?"

"Ooo, *what* is that?" Manny exclaimed, much too excited.

Tori put the bags on the counter and clutched the book to her chest. She sat down in the middle of the couch.

"This is a Memory Book. This is the story of a friendship. I think Manny should get to see this."

Manny and Carrie sat on either side of Tori.

"How old do we get in this?" asked Carrie.

"Just high school graduation, I think."

Tori and Carrie exchanged a meaningful glance.

"Open it up!" said Manny.

A mini-Carrie and a mini-Tori, both with baby fat on their cheeks, along with dripping ice cream cones and toothless smiles, stared back. Manny laughed.

"Now I remember why I don't bring you around my boyfriends," said Carrie.

"Relax, Bitch," said Tori. "Drink your wine."

It had been a while since Carrie had looked at old pictures. She and Tori were different with friend and family photographs. Tori had them framed all over her apartment. Carrie hung abstract canvases instead.

Why was that? Because space is limited? Because the past belongs to the past?

Tori and Manny searched the faces of the fifth-grade class picture.

"That looks like Rachel," said Manny. "Is that possible?"

"Yeah, that's her. She was okay as a kid. We played with her sometimes," said Tori.

Manny looked confused.

"Her parents split up after this year. She and her mom went to live in California. We didn't see her again until high school when she moved back to live with her dad because her mom died," said Carrie.

"She was weird in high school," said Tori. "Never stopped talking about her father."

"Mmm, maybe we could have been more understanding, though. She had just lost her mom," said Carrie. "Maybe she was afraid of losing her Dad, too."

"Do you know why her parents split up?" asked Manny. "Why her mother took her to California?"

Carrie wondered what he knew, if anything. She remembered a rumor. She shook her head.

"Her mom's family lived there."

He nodded. "And it's just about the furthest you can get from here."

He looked back to the book while Tori pointed out Carrie on each page, all the way to high school.

Tori turned the next page, and a pile of loose photos dropped out. They were of Emily when she was young.

"Why are they there?" asked Carrie.

"I don't know," said Tori.

"She looks so much like Carrie, here," said Manny, picking one up.

"I know," said Tori. "Look at her here. When she was young, she looked exactly like Carrie did at the same age."

"She doesn't look like me," said Carrie.

Tori and Manny sorted through the other Emily photos.

"Is this one Carrie, or Emily?" asked Manny.

"She looks like *you*!" Carrie said it way too loud.

Tori and Manny looked up in surprise. Carrie felt tears stinging her eyes and forced them to stay, but one slipped onto her cheek. She quickly wiped it away.

"It's just the damn hormones," she said.

"She looks like both of you. We're done anyway," said Tori, gently. She started to close the album, but Manny stopped her.

"There's another page," he said, pulling the album into his lap.

He opened it and gasped. Carrie strained to see. It was a two-page spread of photographs of Carrie with a belly that grew from barely there to popping out. In the center of the collage stood a very pregnant Carrie, holding her belly, at the edge of the ocean at sunrise.

Manny touched it gently, tracing her silhouette with his finger.

He looked at Tori.

"Thank you," he said, "for taking these pictures."

"I was her coach, you know. It was part of the job."

Manny's eyes glistened. Again he said, "Thank you, Tori."

Carrie wanted to slam the book shut. She tried to just wait it out. Wait until he closed it.

"I need a copy of this one," he said. He took his phone out to take a picture.

"No, no, you don't," said Carrie.

"Look at you," he said. "You're more beautiful pregnant than I ever imagined. And I have a good imagination."

She wanted to tell him just how she had felt, then. She had felt many things, but beautiful was not on the list. He took the picture.

"Don't you have to pick up the food for dinner?" she asked.

He looked at the clock. "You're right," he said. He seemed clueless for once of her feelings. She was grateful for that.

When Manny went to get the take-out, Tori took her hand. "I'm so sorry, Carrie. I honestly thought that album ended at high school."

"It's alright. It's just that all these memories caught me by surprise. It's not the best day for them."

Tori looked sympathetic. "You haven't told him yet, have you?"

"He hasn't asked."

"You know he's not going to ask."

Carrie inhaled, taking a moment. "That sounds a little judgy."

Tori just looked at her. Carrie, in turn, felt sick in her stomach, but Tori squeezed her hand in support.

* * *

Tori left soon after the show, giving Manny a big hug. Carrie knew they had bonded tonight. She was grateful for that.

Emily texted Carrie and Carrie read it to Manny.

**We are leaving NC now.**

**Should be home in the morning.**

**I love you both.**

Manny put his arm around her shoulder. She looked up from the phone into his eyes. She wanted to repeat those words. I love you both, but she held back.

"It wasn't the weekend we thought it was going to be," he said.

"No, it wasn't," she said. "It was perfect."

Manny ran on the edges of the ocean in the morning, before work. The cold lacey water played a game of catching his feet as he ran. Surfers and lone photographers were the only people he saw at that time. Everyone stayed in their own world, with barely a nod to each other. No one was there to talk. They came for the magic of the sun rising and the push and pull of the waves. Every day looked different and felt different, yet every day the same thing happened. The sun always rose and the mystery and magnificence of the ocean waves were always just a footstep away from him.

In the office at Turner Foundation, he also felt like he was running along the edge of a mystery, but one he had no desire to stop and watch. Never before had he wanted so much to stay on the edge, be invisible, and let people forget about him as he did his work.

He'd managed to do that, for the most part. He mostly worked alone and occasionally with Rachel. She brought him the comments from Tom Turner, who he rarely saw, except in meetings with outside firms and businesses.

He looked forward to the night classes he taught, even though it meant long hours. On most days, it was his only time to talk to anyone, to come in from the edge. There he was the one that set the stage for everyone to speak, for everyone to be seen, for everyone to learn.

* * *

Manny's work hours were so long that he and Carrie had to schedule dates to be able to see each other. She was waiting for him at his apartment after his evening class.

"You look so good," he said, kissing her.

"I've missed you," she said, following him up the stairs to his door.

"I've missed you, too. And the kids. Emmie doesn't even text me back half the time. What are they up to?"

"Emily sleeps half the day. Eats, showers, and goes to work. I don't know about the rest of the crew."

Manny put his backpack of books on the floor near the door and led her into the living room.

"Johnny sent me a text today that they were having pizza around 6 pm and would I like to come join them," he said.

"Pizza party at my house? And I wasn't invited?"

"Well, I think it was on the beach. He said there was live music at the bandstand tonight."

"What did you tell him? Did you tell him you had a date with me?"

"I said I was teaching a class, which I was when he texted me."

"Is it weird he invited you?"

"He's never done that before. I'll have to reach out to

him this weekend. And make sure I spend time with Emmie, too."

Carrie nodded. "I don't see any of the gang much. They're all working this summer."

"Things change. Kids get older."

"It's only two weeks until Labor Day. We'll all see each other more after that when you're teaching Fall semester and Emily's summer job at the french fry stand ends."

He forced himself not to frown. He didn't want her to know. His schedule for Fall wouldn't be much better than this. It was true he'd be teaching more then, but his work at Turner wasn't finished yet. The presentation to the public wasn't until October.

"What should we do?" he asked, rubbing his hand along her back. All he wanted to do was lose himself in her arms.

"I've been in the studio all day. Let's go for a walk on the boardwalk," said Carrie.

The moon was bright tonight, hanging low, hovering over the water, as they stepped onto the boardwalk near Manny's place. There was barely anyone on this part of the boardwalk. A few restaurants were small neon dots north on the boardwalk horizon, their music and laughs silenced here.

"It's romantic," said Carrie. "Come here." She tugged his arm and led him down a ramp, but instead of walking to the ocean, she turned to the right.

"This way," she said, "under the boardwalk."

"It's dark in here."

"It's a secret place," she said.

"Where Jersey girls go?"

She laughed. "That's right. Jersey girls do it under the boardwalk. It's where we test the Bennies."

"Am I a Benny?"

"Kiss me and I'll let you know."

He could barely see her as his eyes adjusted to the darkness. He could feel her, though. Her arms wrapped around his neck as her body pressed against him. He ran his hands down her back and kissed her long.

The cool night air and the strong smell of tar and sea spray permeated his skin. He briefly remembered a young Carrie, pulling him under the boardwalk. But he pushed her from his mind. He wanted no one but this woman in his arms, now. She brought him back from the edge; she could see him even in the darkness. With her, he wasn't a shadow avoiding others.

Eventually, they emerged from the wooden cave and sat on a boardwalk bench, looking out at the moon and waves.

"Not a Benny," she said. "You kiss like you belong here."

He looked over, feeling a rush of love for her. She leaned her head back on his arm.

"Y'know, we were talking about you not long ago," she said. "And Johnny asked me why don't you live in the cottage with us."

He smiled at her and played with a strand of her hair.

"You could, if you want," she said.

He said nothing, still playing with her hair. He was afraid to speak and break the spell. Everything in the universe felt perfect. The perfect curls in her hair. The perfect blue eyes that were looking at him. The perfect smile she gave him.

"We could be a family, then," he said, quietly, as if testing if the conversation could be real.

"We could," she said. "I could be the mom."

"And I'll be the dad."

"We'll have a beautiful daughter."

"And her stray friends."

"And we can all eat pizza together," said Carrie.

"And watch live music on the beach."

"And you and I can sleep together," she laughed.

"And wake up together," he said.

"And wake up together."

"I want that, Carrie." Did she know how much he wanted it?

"Let's do it, then," she said.

He gave her a lazy kiss, touching her first so it was barely a kiss, then tasting her more and more. This was all he ever wanted, to kiss her with no rush, no time limit, no reason to prove anything. Just kiss her and savor her. Now, it seemed like he could. Time together was stretching in front of them into a long, lazy future of kisses and pizza and waking up together.

"You'll have to make room for me," he said when they took a break.

"What? I already made room for your toothbrush."

There was barely enough space for his backpack in her room. He hadn't been able to hang a shirt in her closet yet. How was this going to work? He knew they could deal with it, but her cottage was tiny.

"I come with baggage."

She rolled her eyes. "Don't we all? I'll work on it."

There was something else.

"We should do it in steps," he said reluctantly. "I know you need time for your art. I don't want to take space and time you don't have to share. And it's good when Emily spends time with me in my apartment. She and I are still catching up."

"You're right. We'll figure it out. I'll start by purging my closet this weekend while you spend time with her."

He took her hand as they walked back to his place.

Her car was parked near the stairs to his door. He wasn't sure what she wanted. It was getting late and they both had work in the morning.

"Tell me what you want," he said.

"You," she said, pushing him up the stairs.

He laughed and stood still, making her push him hard up each step.

"Open the damn door," she said impatiently when they got to the landing.

"You never ask me what I want," he joked, unlocking it.

"I know what you want," she said.

They were inside the door now. She was standing in front of him, her eyes staring at him, her smile daring him. He wasn't sure he could make it to the bedroom. This was not a joke, this way that he felt for her.

He picked her up and laughed at her surprise. She giggled while he carried her to the bed and dropped her unceremoniously on to the zebra-striped sheets.

"Hey! Gentle! I'm a lady here!"

"A lady? I have to take my clothes off, then?"

He sat down next to her and pulled his shirt over his head, kicking off his sandals. She did the same.

They switched from the joking to the power that pulled them together. He kissed her on the lips but quickly changed to kiss down the side of her neck, into her breasts. He could suck and nibble her nipples all night, listening to her moan, feeling her healing him. Slowly, his hands explored the rest of her.

The straps and remaining pieces of clothing were each a puzzle to remove. Each seemed to take forever, both frustrating him and turning him on in the anticipation. He didn't even try to remove the final bit of lace. It was all that held him back. His fingers returned to the lace again and again, as the sweat and the moans from them both increased. Her nipples were hard on his chest, her mouth and his mouth nibbling into each other. He rubbed his finger against her and felt the moisture seeping through the thin material. She wanted him. He wanted her. He knew this, but still, he had to ask. He wasn't sure he had the strength to speak.

His finger slid gently under the band against her skin and down to her center. She was so wet. He groaned and pulled back. He pulled his finger away, teasing her and himself, then slid slowly down beneath the lace again. This time she arched to him and held his hand, not letting him pull away.

"Tell me what you want," he said into her ear.

"You. All of you," she panted.

"My hand first," he said.

"Yes," she moaned as he explored her then, letting her lead him exactly as she needed him. She pulled the lace down herself, squirming to stay attached to him, hanging on his arm.

Again, he was running on the edge of the lacey waters of Carrie. Running and darting, playing a game that never stopped, that teased them both, that made him marvel at the strength of this miracle, this desire for each other, as strong as the sun rising every day.

He held onto her, feeling her rocking and shuddering, tightening and gasping. She had let him into her world. He didn't have to prove anything to her anymore. He felt his eyes sting with thankfulness.

She moved to the edge of the bed as he put on the condom so that he could stand as he entered her. They both groaned as he did. He ran his hands along her legs, these legs that wrapped him. He kissed them and held them, prolonging the sweet ride.

He stood before her, bringing her everything he had. He fingered her breasts then as he watched her face, until he sensed her giving in to the flow, riding it with shallow breath. Now he was in the waters of Carrie, like a surfer in the pipe, immersed in her beauty. He bent and buried his face into her hair as he held her and came home, full circle, complete, to shore.

It was two days later, during an important meeting at the Turner Foundation when Manny felt his phone vibrate. Then vibrate again a few minutes later. Then again.

He snuck a look, holding it under the large conference table and saw it was from Carrie.

He tried to hide his smile. They had been texting more and more each day. It was becoming harder to get through an hour without sharing a thought, a photo, a joke, a desire with each other. Now, she was calling instead of texting, though. He only half-listened to a representative of a fast-food chain speaking. His thoughts instead imagined what Carrie wanted to tell him. How much did she want him this morning? Soon they would wake up almost every morning next to each other. He wondered if the texts would slow down then or increase.

He called her as soon as he could after the meeting when he had privacy.

"Manny!"

There was panic in her voice. Something clenched inside his chest. He swallowed, waiting.

"I don't know where Emily is. I think she ran away!"

"No, that doesn't sound right. Why do you think that?"

"Her stuff is gone. Her backpack, some of her clothes, her journal, her laptop, her chargers, toothbrush. She's gone."

"Maybe there's a note you missed?"

"No. She's not responding to my calls and texts. And I know what it's about. It's that damn Johnny. He took her someplace."

"I think he would make sure she asked you first. That boy is scared of you."

"Yeah, well, he should be scared. There's more. There's way more. I found them in the morning, in Emily's bedroom. He was sleeping in her bed! I freaked out on him and her too. Told him to get out and stay out of here. I saw him leave, but then I had to teach an art class. I've got to go now and teach another. But looks like the first chance she got, she went off with him."

"I'll get in touch with them," he said. "I'll find out what happened."

"What?" Carrie was raising her voice. "I just told you what happened. Do you not believe me, or do you just not want to interfere? How can you be so calm?"

He waited a few seconds. It was easy for him to be calm like it was easy for her not to be. He got calmer when it was needed. It didn't mean he wasn't feeling like his heart was being ripped out of his chest, right now. Now wasn't the time to tell Carrie about missing Indigenous women, about MMIW. Calmly, get the information. Then get Emily back home before anything can happen to her.

"When you say sleeping, Carrie, do you mean he was just sleeping? What did you see?"

"I know what I saw!"

"Exactly, tell me exactly what you saw."

"Exactly. He was sound asleep and she had just taken a shower and was dressed, combing her hair. His car was parked beyond the house, so I wouldn't be able to see it while I was here. I don't know what time he came here, it was after I went to bed around midnight, but it wasn't this morning and I wasn't born yesterday."

"Maybe he just needed a place to stay last night."

"How can you be so!" Carrie stopped suddenly. She sighed.

"Emmie always tells me they're just friends, that's there's nothing romantic going on. Did she tell you something else?" he asked.

"She doesn't have to. I know that friends fuck too."

"God, Carrie."

"It's just truth, Manny."

He knew she was right. But he couldn't believe Johnny would do it with Carrie in the house.

"Let me just try to get in touch with them, okay?" he asked.

"Alright," she said. "Alright, but please, Manny, just promise me, you'll let me know if you hear from her?"

"I will. Go ahead, teach your class. I'll take care of it."

* * *

He expected Emily to answer his calls and texts immediately. Two hours later, he still blamed the spotty reception on the Hook for her silence. Instead of lunch, he drove off the Hook, closer to a cell tower. Again he called and texted.

Still, there was no response from neither Emily nor Johnny.

That was the first he realized maybe she didn't want to talk to him either. It wasn't only Carrie she had run away from. He was the other half of home. She had run away from him, too.

He was standing at an overlook park. He could see Sandy Hook, stretching beneath him towards lower Manhattan. The city sparkled in the sun and water, like a silver shimmer. There was a time years ago when he had stood here and watched the Twin Towers glow as bright as the afternoon sun, then slowly turn to orange as it set. There was a time that Emily would answer him on the first ring.

Everything changes.

He could see cars, like toys, riding the single road down the middle of the Hook. He had driven that road when he came here, full of anticipation, full of hope for a new relationship with Emily and Carrie. He had even dreamed they could be a family together. And where was that dream now? Broken. He couldn't help feeling like it was due to him coming here and disrupting the balance that Carrie and Emily had had together.

He needed to get back to work. There was another meeting that would take up the whole afternoon. He looked at the scroll of texts he'd sent Emily this morning. They were all demands for her to contact him or Carrie. What did it come down to? He had lost sight of it. His parents had never demanded anything of him. There were only two things he really needed to say. He typed into the phone.

**I love you and I trust you Em.**

She replied right away.

**I love you too Daddy.**

His eyes stung as he drove back to the Hook.

* * *

Manny drove to Carrie's house as soon as work was over for the day. She came out of the door and stood at the top of the porch steps when she heard his truck.

"Did you hear from her?"

"She's okay, Carrie. I'm sure of it."

Carrie raised her voice, "Did you hear from her?"

"Yes, I heard from her."

"Well, what did she say?"

He hesitated and looked away, not sure how Carrie would take it.

"She said she loved me."

"What else?"

"Nothing else. It was a text."

He looked at her then. She exhaled. Then sank, deflated, and sat on the step beneath her. She stared straight ahead.

He sat down next to her and put his arm around her. She sat still, frozen, staring ahead.

"I'm a failure," she said.

"You're not a failure."

"I'm a failure as a mother."

"That doesn't make sense. You gave her life. You gave her food and shelter. You taught her to respect others and the earth and the sea. You've been a good mother, such a good mother."

"But I failed when it came to teaching her this."

"This? What?"

"How to make important decisions. How to not ruin your life."

He shook his head, no. "She hasn't ruined her life. Besides, this is her path, not yours. We just have to trust her. That she'll figure it out and come back."

"But my heart is breaking, Manny."

"Mine is too," he said, but that wasn't the full truth. His whole body felt broken.

She stood up, dusting the sand off herself. "I can't just give up on her. She's underage. She's a baby. We're going to have to call the police and report her missing."

"No, no. Calling the police can backfire, Carrie. Johnny could get into a mess of trouble and..." He couldn't tell Carrie, but Rachel would certainly seize on the story to use against Carrie, somehow. "Please, not the police. It's not like she's been kidnapped. We know she's with Johnny. It hasn't even been twenty four hours. Let me try again to talk to them."

"I don't know how much longer I can wait. I'm going bananas here, alone, waiting for a call. Will you stay here, then?"

"I was thinking I should go back to my place, in case they go there. Emmie has a key."

She nodded, looking into the distance, away from him. "You're right. You should go. And I should stay here in case they come back here. I'll call Tori and ask her to stay over."

"That's a good idea. I'm going to go," he said. He gave her a warm hug and she held onto him. He pulled back and gave her a soft kiss on the lips.

"Trust me," he said. "I'll take care of it." He wasn't sure his words convinced him or her.

He walked back to his car. She was still standing in the same spot when he drove away.

* * *

At his apartment, Manny called Johnny's foster mother.

"He ain't here anymore," she said. "He turned 18 the other day. So, that's that. I told him he had to leave. He doesn't want to live in my house and I don't want him either. He's probably living in that car he bought."

"But he's still in high school. Can't he go to another foster home?"

"You have to ask him that. Some kids get to stay in the system until they're 21, but I wouldn't let them stay in my home. The older they get, the less they listen to me. Anyway, he went and signed the papers that he doesn't want their help anymore."

As soon as Manny hung up he texted Johnny. That kid needed some family.

**Let's make it a happy birthday. You can live with me now Johnny. Come home with Emily.**

He got up from the couch and went into the kitchen where his metalsmith tools were set up. He sat down and pulled out a new square of copper, placing his phone nearby. He drew a large oval, big enough for a belt buckle. He had no plan for this. He just wanted to bang the seconds away, waiting. He wasn't mad at Johnny. He was mad at himself. He hadn't realized the kid's plea when he told him his birthday was coming up. He had brushed Johnny's request to see him aside. That pizza party was probably his birthday party. Manny drew a rising sun, over water, on the inside of the oval. The sun rising in the East over the ocean. Johnny needed a birthday gift.

It was hours later when he heard the little bell of text received. It was not from Johnny but Emily.

**Daddy do you mean it?**

**Yes. Call me. I have to talk to you or your mom is going to call the police.**

The phone buzzed.

"Emmie. What's going on?"

"Mom threw us out."

"She wasn't throwing you out and she wouldn't have thrown Johnny out if she knew he had no home."

"She thought the worst of us, Dad. We're just friends. We weren't doing anything. She doesn't even trust me. Sometimes I really hate her. All she does is play with her paint or go off with you or her friends. She doesn't even know who I am. She doesn't realize how grown up I am."

"I know you're grown up. So you understand, we can work this out. We'll all sit down together and figure it out. I just need you to come home."

"I don't want to live with her anymore."

He didn't hesitate, even though he knew what it would mean. "Come live with me, then. Both you and Johnny."

"She's going to be mad at you, Dad."

"I know, but you and Johnny can't be out there, homeless. She'll understand that."

"What if she doesn't, Dad? I need to know if you're on my side or hers."

"There aren't any sides, Emily. This is family, this is a circle. We're all in this together. Your mom knows that."

"I'll talk to Johnny about it," she sniffled. "I'll call you back later, Dad."

* * *

Manny called Carrie and updated her on what he had learned about Johnny being homeless.

"What? Why didn't they tell us that?" she said.

"I think he tried to tell me, but I didn't realize it. I guess we haven't been paying much attention to them."

"Still, Emily didn't need to go with him."

"She's mad at you, Carrie. I'm just saying. I'm not judging, okay? I'm just letting you know what's happening. When she comes back, looks like, she'll be staying with me."

"What?"

He knew she had heard him. He wasn't going to repeat it.

"And where will you be?"

"I'll be where Emily needs me to be. I'll be at my apartment for now."

He heard her sigh.

"We'll get through it," he said.

"You're letting a fifteen-year-old pull all your strings, Manny."

"I don't know what else to do, Carrie. I was hoping you would understand."

"I do understand," she said. Her voice was gentle. "I'm on the same team. Team Emily. You do whatever you need to do to get her back safe, Manny."

Manny called in for a personal day the next morning. He went to meet Johnny's social worker.

The waiting room was full of mostly women, babies and young kids. The women looked away from him, but the kids came right up, curious. One little guy in a superhero shirt stood in front of him for a long time, staring.

"Hey," said Manny.

"Are you my daddy?" said the hero.

He looked in those big eyes, not wanting to say no. "I wish," he whispered.

The mom grabbed her son. "Leave that man alone!"

"You told me I'd see him today."

"Shh. He's not here."

The social worker told Manny she couldn't share any information with him due to privacy laws.

"Can I just ask you, then, in general, is this normal, that kids get turned out as soon as they're 18, out onto the street?"

"No, it's not. It's different in every state but in New Jersey, we're now able to extend the services until 21 if certain criteria are met. Johnny really needs to contact me. Unfortunately, he also has an option of refusing my help now, since he's an adult."

"What about when these kids turn 21 or don't meet the extension criteria? Or, like him, just don't want to be in the system anymore? Are there nonprofits that help them?"

"There are a few, I've heard about some. But, unfortunately, there aren't any in our county. There's a real need for one around here."

* * *

Manny drove back to his apartment, hoping to see Johnny's car, but the lot was empty. He had no classes to teach tonight.

He sat on the couch and the weight of the day came down upon him. He couldn't shake the image of those kids staring at him. His dad was hardly around when he was growing up. He saw himself in those little kids today. It made him think of his brothers.

He picked up his phone. Cochi's voice was strong and familiar.

"Hey, brother," said Cochi.

"Hey."

"So, how's the big sugar daddy doing? You keeping everybody happy?"

Manny managed to laugh. "No. The exact opposite. Emily ran away."

"What? No! Why would she do that?"

"It has to do with her friend, Johnny. Plus, I'm afraid that I've come between her and Carrie too much. Maybe I should have stayed away."

"No, you don't believe that. I know you. Hey, I know what a good dad you are, you took care of me and Little-Bro when you were just a kid. I've seen you with Emily. You can't do anything wrong in her eyes."

"Well, maybe that's part of the problem. She only sees the good in me and it makes her imagine she sees the worst in Carrie. They aren't getting along."

They sat in silence for a minute.

"I'll try calling Emmie. We talk sometimes," said Cochi.

"I've been wondering what you've been telling her."

"Hey, I'm the cool uncle. I tell her stories about my wonderful life on the road, singing in all the best venues, coast to coast."

"Every gin mill with an extra 2 feet for a microphone stand?"

"She only sees the good in me, too."

"I'd be grateful for you to call her."

"Yeah, hey, I've meant to call you anyway. I'm going to be in your neighborhood soon. We got a gig in Asbury Park. Have you ever heard of it?"

Manny laughed. "Yeah, I've heard of it."

* * *

Manny took a shower to clean himself of the doubts and sadness. He tried to put his mind in the right place, to be thankful for all that he had, for all that he could give. He could give to those kids in the waiting room. Maybe not those kids specifically, but kids like Johnny, he could help them. There was no fairness in life. The only fairness is what you can do to make the world better.

He went to the beach and walked alone along the water. The ocean soothed him. The ocean heard his prayers. The ocean gave him hope. He went home and then he heard the bell of a text from Emily.

**We will be at your apt in an hour.**

On Saturday, Carrie watched from the porch as Manny drove up in his truck and Johnny drove up in his junk-mobile. She stood with her arms crossed, watching. She bit her lower lip.

Emily got out of Johnny's car and walked up the steps. Emily didn't look at Carrie but held her head high.

"I came to get some clothes to bring to Dad's."

"Don't let me stop you. Looks like you're running the show now."

Carrie knew she sounded like a bitch. Why couldn't she just tell Emily she loved her and she was happy to see her back again? Instead, she bit her lower lip again, even though that didn't seem to stop her words.

Emily walked quickly into the house.

Manny walked up the porch steps and stood next to Carrie. His face, as always, was so calm. She looked over to Johnny.

He got out of his car with both hands up.

"Mrs. Mom, I'm sorry. I told Emmie not to come with me, but she wouldn't let me go without her."

"Put your hands down. I'm not going to shoot you."

He hesitated.

"I don't have a gun."

That convinced him. Still, he stayed his distance.

"That was a stupid thing to do, y'know," she said. "You could have explained it to me. I would have let you stay if I had known."

"Yeah, uh, I guess so. You didn't act like you wanted to talk when you kicked me out."

"You're right," she smiled a little. "It's alright, Johnny. Manny and I talked about it. We're going to help you get on your feet, okay?"

He nodded his head. "Yeah, he told me. It's awesome. Thanks."

Johnny came closer to them.

"Johnny, I didn't tell you, I talked to your social worker," said Manny.

"Who? Miss Sullivan? She's not my social worker anymore. I'm out of the system now."

"She says that's not entirely true. She needs to talk to you about the details. You might have more options than you thought. But the most important thing is, she has your records. There's information on your parents in them."

Johnny looked up. That had gotten his attention.

"Does she know anything about my father?"

Manny sighed. "She couldn't tell me, but she can tell you."

Johnny turned his head and gazed into the distance. "I'm not sure I want to know," he said.

"That's understandable. I can go with you, if you want, to her office," said Manny. "It's important decisions to make. I can help you discuss it with her."

"Would you? I hate that place. It's so confusing."

Manny nodded. "I know. I spent four hours in the waiting room."

"You did? You did that for me? Thanks. I guess we made you guys worry a lot."

This time, biting her lip helped. Johnny didn't need any grief from her. He had enough.

Manny patted Johnny on the shoulder. "It's over," he said.

They could hear Emily banging drawers and doors.

"Not over yet," said Carrie. "I'm going in there."

Manny looked at her, cautioning her with his eyes.

"Don't worry. I dialed my Bitch level down. Let's see how it works."

Emily was stuffing clothes into shopping bags. Carrie forced herself to speak in a measured tone.

"Emily, I'm glad to see that you're back and that you're okay. I was really worried about you."

"No, you weren't. I'm sure you were happy I was gone." Emily glared at Carrie, her face full of challenge.

Again, Carrie tried to speak carefully. "Why do you say that? Why would I be happy if you were gone?"

"Because then you'd have much more time with your art and your girlfriends and my Dad. You're never around anymore. All I am is a nuisance to you now."

"I don't understand what you mean. I'm here all the time, all day. I work here. I run the classes and do my art here. I don't leave for days at a time."

"Yeah, when you're home, you don't want to talk because your head is into your current recycled trash collage A-R-T and when you go places, you don't take me."

"You never want to go with me! Every time I ever ask you, you say no. You're always with Johnny and the other kids."

"Well, because I need to be around somebody! Mom, don't roll your eyes at me! You always do that! You have no respect for me! Why are you rolling your eyes at me? You don't respect me!"

"Respect? Really? You want to talk about respect? How about respecting your mother? How about not running away, letting her think you're kidnapped or in an accident or horrible things, Em? Not answering her texts or calls. That was just, mean. That was really mean, you wouldn't even text me."

"I texted Dad."

"I'm glad that you did that, but it hurt, Em."

"You just won't let it go, will you? You see the worst in everybody. Dad sees the best in them. That's why I hate you. I'm done here. I'm going back to the apartment with Johnny."

"Wait, this makes no sense. How long are you going to stay there?"

"I don't know."

"School's starting soon. You need to be here."

"Johnny will drive me to school."

Carrie followed her to the hallway and watched her go to Johnny's car. That hadn't gone well.

Manny was watching her. Carrie shook her head. "I tried," she said.

She went into her bedroom and flopped on her bed, on her back.

"I'm exhausted and hurt. She's pushing me to my limits and I'm really missing you, Manny."

He laid down next to her, his face above hers. "We got our girl back," he said.

She smiled. "You got our girl back. She hates me. She doesn't want anything to do with me."

"She will. It's a teenage thing, right?"

"Yeah, I guess so. I know my Mom and I both went through hell when I was her age. Emmie's lucky she's got you." She put her hand on his arm.

"You've got me too."

God, he was good-looking. His calm face was so soothing.

"I know, in theory, I do. But you're not here in my bed at night."

He ran his finger over her body. "I'm here now."

She smiled slightly. She closed her eyes and concentrated on his finger, running along her body. But she couldn't stop thinking of Emily.

"Do you really have the time, now?" she asked.

"What is time? Time is all around us." He continued running his finger slowly over her body. "The sun is shining. When it's gone, the moon will shine. There's always time."

"Always time. I want you, Manny, but this isn't the right time." She shook her head and sat up, holding his hand that had been trailing her body.

"Okay," he said. He stood up and she stood next to him.

Was it really okay with him? He was always so calm. How would she tell if it wasn't okay with him?

"I'll leave and let you rest," he said. "I should get back to the kids anyway. But call me if you need to talk, okay?"

Was that his way of saying that he needed to talk? He never asked her for anything.

"I will. I'll call," she whispered.

* * *

On Monday morning, Carrie woke before dawn and could not get back to sleep in her empty house. She got out of bed and slipped into yesterday's clothes. She put on an extra sweatshirt and grabbed her camera. She could sleep later.

Since she was awake before dawn, she would take pictures of the sun rising over the ocean. She often used her photos as inspiration for paintings. She drove to the farthest spot north, to the place where the Hook just began to bend. The Manhattan skyline was still a string of lights, barely visible today. The sand was cold and wet on her bare feet.

It was a foggy and mist-filled morning created by the changing temperatures of late summer. There was an ethereal soft, white, natural filter on everything. It was so magical. She wondered how she could paint this feeling. She wandered, following each scene that caught her eye, clicking on the camera. A cooing sound of mourning doves, so mournful and haunting, led her further. She found them together on the grass, eating breakfast, singing to each other. They ignored her as she took their picture.

She turned a corner and looked down Officers Row, a line of mansions that once housed Army officials. She was surprised to see Manny's truck parked in front of one of the houses.

Why was he here? It was on the other side of the Hook from her cottage. It must be his work. He'd never mentioned he worked in one of these houses. She thought he was working in a large building nearby where she knew the University held Oceanography classes. She realized he'd never told her exactly where he worked. She had just assumed. But why was he here so early?

She angled closer to the row, positioning so that she would have the best shot of the line of identical houses, with the morning sun that was now lighting each porch to a golden glow. It was through the lens of the camera that she saw Manny stepping out of one of the front doors. She was just about to click when Rachel came into view. He held the door open for her. They walked to the street. Manny opened the door of what must be Rachel's car, parked behind his truck. Rachel got in and Manny closed the door for her. He was always such a gentleman. He waved as she pulled away.

Carrie stepped back into the shadows of a tree. Manny, in his truck, drove away too.

She looked at her watch. It was 7 am.

*There is always time.*

She took a deep breath. It was nothing, she told herself. Birds called loudly to each other. Some were screeching. Some were crying. It was such relentless noise. She could barely think. Damn birds. She jogged towards her car to get away from the noise.

Could she have made such a mistake? Could she have read him so wrong? No, she answered. He's in love with me. He's a good man. I need to trust him. He'll have an explanation.

Really? An explanation for leaving a house with another woman, one that was always by his side, when he first moved here? Just what went on between Manny and Rachel? She never did understand that. He had never offered any explanation. What was going on now?

All day, she heard the voices inside her arguing. She couldn't concentrate on her work.

* * *

The next morning she met Tori on the beach. They had joined as volunteers on the Clean Beach Committee. The organization ran routine beach sweeps that sorted and counted every bit of litter. The data was used for studies that showed effects of changes in the environment and Park policy. Carrie hoped it could be used to predict how commercialization on the Hook would harm the environment.

Tori stabbed a cigarette butt with the trash picker. "You're going to have to ask him, Carrie. Confront him with it so you can find out the truth."

"I know I should just do that, but it's embarrassing. It shouldn't bother me so much to see him talking to another woman. What is wrong with me? I sound like a jealous teenager."

"Aren't you jealous, though? Isn't that what's bothering you?"

Carrie, wearing gloves, picked up two empty beer bottles and added them to her bag.

"Am I jealous? No. I feel more hurt than jealous. I'm not jealous if that's who he is, I'm just disappointed. So disappointed, Tori. Disappointed in myself for trusting him."

"Wait, wait. Don't jump to conclusions. He's so devoted to you and Emily. It's not like he flirts with other women."

"He flirted when we were in college. He always had that big, sexy smile on his face, always so friendly to every girl that looked at him. I thought he was different now. Maybe he's just better at hiding it now."

"Or maybe he just grew up. I tend to believe it has something to do with his work, out there on the Hook. That would make some sense, right?"

"Maybe. He never talks about what he's doing. Just said it's research for the University."

"Right. Maybe he has to work with Rachel, and he hasn't told you, because, well, you know you'd go all Jersey on him, wouldn't you?"

Carrie managed to laugh a little. "That's true. He avoids my drama whenever he can."

"He's a smart man. We know this."

"Yes, we know this."

They rounded a bend to a new stretch of beach. They were on the river side and a dozen boats were anchored just offshore. Remains of a party from the night before were obvious. There were styrofoam containers from local restaurants everywhere, some with half-eaten shrimp. Carrie picked up a bottle of tabasco sauce. Piles of clam shells and lemon wedges were thrown around a circle of burnt charcoal.

"Pigs!" said Carrie, glaring at the boats.

"They think it's their private playground," said Tori. She picked up a bottle. "Champagne? Really?"

"They're not even supposed to be here," said Carrie. "The Park closes at dark, no camping allowed. I hate that they think the laws don't apply to them. I really hate them." She looked towards the boats again, her face scrunched at the sight.

*You always see the worst in people.* Emily had yelled it at her.

She didn't want to see the worst.

She wanted only to see the world like she had seen it through the camera lens at dawn. There was beauty in everything. The fog and the mourning doves. The mist and the surf. An opening door and a rising sun. Manny's face in the morning. But Rachel had appeared suddenly, like these private boats on the water. It felt wrong. Rachel didn't fit there.

Why? Carrie was missing something. Why did Manny allow Rachel in his world? She was going to have to ask him.

"Your work is changing," said Ann, the owner of the gallery in Asbury Park. Carrie had brought her a dozen new paintings.

"I think so, too," said Carrie. "I'm not sure if it's for better or worse, though."

She immediately regretted saying it. She had just set herself up to hear a critique.

"It's different. There's less movement. But there are more layers." Ann stood back, looking them all over. "You're showing us more of you. It's getting deeper."

Ann slowly walked down the line of paintings leaning against the wall. Carrie saw every flaw in each of them as she watched. Ann stopped and looked back at them.

"There's always been some mystery behind your art, always making us wonder what's driving it. And it IS driven. Now it feels, we're close to understanding. Just one more layer and the mystery will be revealed. It's exciting to watch your art progress."

Carrie felt a chill. It all suddenly felt invasive.

"Mona Lisa never revealed her mystery," said Carrie.

"True, but she wasn't the artist. It was DaVinci that revealed her. She was *his* mystery."

Carrie thought of the painting she had started with Manny's face. She still hadn't let anyone see it, not even Tori. She looked at her canvases against the wall. The one at home was better than any of them. But it wasn't finished. There was something more she needed to add.

"Maybe the next batch will have my masterpiece." She forced a laugh to sound lighthearted.

"I'm counting on it," said Ann. "But these are wonderful. We need to give you your own show."

"When?" asked Carrie.

"Sometime in the new year? I'm going over next year's schedule with my partner today. I'll get back to you on the dates. How long do you think it will take to put about 20 paintings together?"

"Probably by February," said Carrie. The month of Emily's birthday and Valentine's Day. She wondered where she and Manny would be by then. Would her new paintings reflect their relationship?

* * *

Carrie left the gallery and took a walk on the boardwalk, looking for a stand to buy an iced coffee. She was so busy reading the menu signs that she was startled when she felt her arm grabbed.

Manny laughed at her surprise.

"Hello, lady," he said.

She saw him for a second as a stranger, so incredibly handsome with such a warm smile just for her. She smiled back at him.

"What are you doing here?" she said.

It took him only a second to answer, but she sensed a delay.

"I'm here a lot. I take my classes here all the time."

She looked around.

"Where's the class?"

He looked around as if he lost them. "Not here."

She questioned him with her eyes.

He smiled mysteriously.

"You're hiding something," she said.

He laughed and took her hand. "It's nothing. I come here all the time. Are you hungry? Let's go eat."

"No, just some iced coffee for me. You eat if you're hungry. I'll watch."

"I already had lunch. For just coffee - I know just the place." He led her down a side street to a perfect little cafe she'd never seen. "Tell me what is happening with you today," he said when they were seated at a bistro table in the cool, dark interior.

"I just met with Ann at the gallery and brought her new paintings. She wants to give me a solo show."

"That's wonderful! When?"

Carrie loved his enthusiasm. His support was so genuine. She loved that about him.

"I don't know exactly. I should be more excited, but whew...she was critiquing my newest work and I was a bundle of nerves. I need some time to recover from that."

He covered her hand on the table with his and gently gave a squeeze. "I know what that's like. Take your time."

"I don't remember you ever getting bad critiques in Art School," she said. "I thought all the professors loved you and your work."

Manny looked at the wall opposite them. It was covered

in paintings by local artists. "It just took one professor," he said.

"What? To make you change your major?"

He nodded.

"Who?" Carrie ran through a mental list of the professors that they had shared. "Oh my god, Manny. Did you let that creepy oil painting guy make you stop painting and change your major? Change your life?"

"Everything worked out. It was a good lesson for me. To know what some people would think of my work."

"What did he say?"

Manny laughed. "I wasn't giving him what he expected. It wasn't about my technique. It was about my subjects."

"What do you mean? Like what?"

"He kept pushing me to paint more Native subjects, to be more true to my identity, but he had no idea what that really means. I did a still life. It was just a bunch of snack foods thrown on a table. Not in a bowl, like fruit, like a Cezanne. Some bags ripped open, spilling over. Pretzels, candy, chips. He tried to tell me I wasn't being honest with myself. We got in an argument. I told him it was the most honest painting I'd ever done."

"What the hell was he looking for?"

"Who knows? Dreamcatchers, probably. Something that had nothing to do with me, only his perception of me. He gave me a C for the class."

"That bastard."

"It's all good. It made me think hard about what I was doing. Art is subjective and the Art world is white, especially back then. It made me realize, my scholarships, a career, would always be in jeopardy if I stayed in a field that was so subjective."

"That's why you switched to Architecture?"

"Partly. I had taken an intro class in it, the same semester. The professor for that happened to be a person of color. He could see I was struggling with the culture shock of being in a place where my identity was constantly being questioned. He reached out and went the extra mile for me. He made a difference. I think I would have quit college after freshman year if it wasn't for him and Rachel."

"Rachel?"

"She took that class too. We both liked it. And I told her how I'd like to change my major, but I was afraid of losing my scholarship. She told me that if I needed money, her father would give me a loan, no problem."

Carrie shook her head. She wondered how many loans, at what interest rate, had Rachel handed out in college. Rachel and her dad never seemed to miss an opportunity to make more money.

"Tom Turner gave you a student loan?"

"No, no. I didn't end up needing it. I worked hard and I kept the scholarship. But just knowing that I had a loan option enabled me to make the change. I'm still so grateful that Rachel offered that."

Carrie thought of Emily yelling how she always sees the worst in people.

"That was nice of her," she managed to say.

"I'm pretty sure she had a hand in getting me the job at the University, too."

"Really?" was all Carrie could say now. The image of Rachel and Manny in the early misty morning a few days before came sharply into her mind. Rachel just kept on giving.

She pulled her hand away from his and pushed her straw into the coffee ice.

"Speaking of Rachel, is there something else you need to tell me?"

"I don't know." He searched her face as if looking for a clue. "You're looking for something specific," he said. "I don't know what it is."

They stared at each other. He did look like he had no idea.

"I saw you, three days ago, in the morning, at 7 am, coming out of one of the Officer Row houses, with Rachel. Can you explain that?"

He smiled with what looked like exaggerated relief.

"I'm so glad. Now you know. You finally figured it out! I'm wildly in love with Rachel and her shining lips and her perfume that makes me sneeze and her high heels that mean she can't walk on grass or sand and ... "

He was laughing. Rachel wasn't his type at all. Carrie knew this.

She punched his arm playfully.

"Stop. Explain," she said.

He grinned. "I needed some files and plans that are stored there," he said. "At least I thought they were there, but it turned out they weren't. Rachel had the keys and met me there."

"Why so early?"

"It was the only time she could be there. She had a flight or something. I thought it was weird too, but I agreed to it because I'm up early anyway."

"It was for your work?"

"Yes."

He stopped smiling. He never told her about his work. She realized maybe because she never asked, because she didn't want to know.

"Part of my work is researching all the buildings on the Hook," he said. "Rachel has access to the buildings. I have to work with her. It's my job, Carrie."

So, Tori was right. It was just Manny doing his job. Carrie put her hand on his. "Part of me knew it was nothing and part of me just wanted to react, to rage."

"It's okay. You didn't rage. I think we've come a long way."

"I sat here and talked to you," she said, amazed at herself. "I think you're rubbing off on me, in a good way, Manny."

He looked at her hand on his and rubbed it with his thumb. "You're rubbing off on me, too."

"Really? I haven't seen you banging doors and yelling."

"It's your passion for your art that inspires me. I don't think you have any idea how much that inspires me. Your passion is for painting. Mine is architecture. I want to create and recreate spaces - homes. I've lost sight of that with teaching. And now, things aren't that great at work. Anyway, I'm looking into it - how I can set up an architect practice here. That's because of you, showing me to follow that passion inside."

"What? Wow. That's a surprise. That's great. I mean, it's not great this new job isn't what you hoped, but if that pushes you to follow the bliss, then, it's all good, right?"

He nodded solemnly and took her hand to his lips, kissing it. "It's all good," he said.

It felt more than all good. It felt very, very good. Setting up a practice here was an investment in time. He sounded ready to stay around after Emily went off to college. She couldn't help but smile.

"So, since you're being so open today," she said, "can

you tell me why you were here before we ran into each other?"

A mysterious grin spread on his face. "No," he said.

She glared at him, but not a real glare. She sensed it was something good.

"Just trust me," he said, like a challenge.

"I need a girl's night out," said Carrie into her phone the next day.

"I am here for you," said Tori.

"Emily's off the streets. Manny has a night class and I won't see him for days."

"None of which matters, anyway. You deserve it all on your own."

"I do, right? I need it." Carrie looked out at the ocean horizon from her doorway. That water flowed all the way to Europe. Sometimes living here made her feel so isolated.

"You are preaching to the choir here, girl. The only thing you need to tell me is when and where," said Tori.

"Asbury Park. 6 pm at the Boardwalk Club."

"Excellent choice, madam."

* * *

Carrie found Tori and a few other girlfriends right on time on the hot summer night.

"Rum buckets all around," yelled Carrie. Rum buckets

were plastic sand pails full of a spicy Rum Punch. They were delicious and a little too easy to drink.

A four-piece band played surf music. An assortment of Adirondack chairs and picnic tables sat on the sand. The group had taken over a circle of chairs. The band played on a nearby stage made of wooden pallets, with the ocean waves pounding on a rock jetty, just a few yards away. It was the perfect setting for summer fun.

Carrie let the music flow through her. She danced with her friends in the sand. It felt so good. She loved surf music. Everyone tried to outdo each other by dancing silly - the fish, the twist, the whatever. They laughed at each other, without caring what anyone else thought. The band sent them love and solos.

Carrie felt the bass like it was deep inside her. She shook her head and danced.

Tori, always the athlete, did a backflip but lost her balance as she landed and sprawled into the sand. Everyone was on their second rum bucket by now. No one could stop laughing. A group of Bennies seated nearby toasted them, holding their rum buckets in the air.

"We need to slow down," said Carrie. She took a walk into the bar's adjacent building.

* * *

Later, Carrie found herself sitting at the inside bar. She knew she was talking sloppy, but couldn't seem to correct herself.

"My boyfriend," she said. "No, my uh, my baby. No, my baby's daddy, he's got tattoos too."

"Really?" said the dude sitting next to her. "So, you like guys with tattoos?"

She nodded her head and sipped on her straw. She reached over and traced the lines on the inked swirl that emerged from the sleeve of his t-shirt.

"Yeah, I like tattoos. You have some serious muscles going on."

"I work out every day. You've got pretty nice muscles yourself." He eyed her breasts in the scooped neck top.

"Haha. I work out too," she said.

Tori grabbed her, pulling her off the barstool.

"Excuse us," Tori said to the dude, then looked at Carrie. "We're taking you home, sister."

"What are you doing? I was just talking to him."

"Too many rum buckets for you, girlfriend. I'm cutting you off."

"I hate you," she said, pouting.

Tori took Carrie's purse from the barstool and put it on Carrie's shoulder.

"Well, hate me then. You'll love me in the morning. Come on, walk with me."

"Bye, dude," waved Carrie.

Dude smiled. "Get home safe."

Walking was a little tricky. Carrie leaned on Tori.

"What the hell were you doing, flirting with that guy?"

"I wasn't flirting. I was talking about Manny."

Tori laughed. "You're drunk and in love. Let's go over to the hotel lobby and get a cab."

"You're right. I'm a love drunk. Not a nasty drunk, not a mean drunk, just a love drunk."

They walked to the nearby boutique hotel. A movie was showing on the rooftop deck, against the brick of the chimney. It looked like a drive-in theatre in the sky. They could see it from the ground as they walked towards the building entrance.

"Oh," said Carrie. "My favorite! *Beach Blanket Bingo!* Let's go see it!"

"Alright, but you have to behave. And no more drinks for you, promise?"

"I promise."

The elevator door opened to the rooftop patio covered in grass carpet.

"This looks fun," said Tori.

There were groupings of chairs and tables. Piles of warm blankets were available in case anyone was cold from the night air. A bar served beer, wine and popcorn. Tori got a wine for herself. They found an open set of chairs and sat down.

"I always loved these movies, with the surfers and the motorcycle gangs," said Carrie.

A scene came on with Frankie and Annette surfing and singing. Carrie got up to dance. There was laughter from the audience. She didn't give a damn what these people thought of her. Two women got up laughing and danced too.

When the movie was over, they walked around the roof, looking out to the ocean, lights, boardwalk and buildings.

"Oh, look at this view, Tori!"

"It's beautiful, isn't it? I love this town."

"Live music, ocean waves, good food, what's not to like?" said Carrie.

"I know," said Tori. "I love it. I'm thinking of getting an apartment down here when my lease is up in a few months."

"Really? That would be fun. You know I want to move here someday, too. Maybe when Emily's older."

"What the hell is going on with Emily, anyway?"

Carrie shook her head. "She won't talk to me."

"I'm sorry," said Tori.

"It's okay," said Carrie. "We'll deal with it. We'll get past it. We just need to learn how to talk to each other."

"Manny had good timing, coming to live here."

"He's better at all this than I thought he would be," said Carrie.

"He obviously has a superpower," said Tori.

"I figured it out. Empathy. That's his superpower."

Carrie looked over the night landscape. "I'm sorry if I'm being a bore about my boyfriend on a girl's night out."

"You know I'd tell you to shut up if I didn't want to hear it," said Tori. "So, tell me. Do you feel like this is it, he's really the one? That this is love?"

"It's not that simple to see. There's a million colors in the shadows."

"A million colors in the shadows? Is that an artist thing? Translation, please."

"Yellow. It's yellow now. I'm yellow, but it doesn't mean I'm in the light."

Tori still look confused.

"I'm happy now," said Carrie. "But that doesn't mean I'm in love. It just means I'm happy, right?"

"You're yellow?"

"I try to talk without colors."

"It's okay. I think I get it," said Tori. "But wait. How do you know, when you're painting, if you're in the shadow or the light?"

Carrie thought about it. "I step back," she said.

"Okay. Step back, then. And tell me if you're in love."

Carrie laughed. "You make it sound so easy. Wait! Isn't that what girl's night out is all about? Stepping back?"

Tori smiled. "Well? How's the view?"

Carrie looked up into the night sky full of stars and neon signs.

"I'm blinded by the light!" she yelled. She raised her hand in the air. "Toast to girl's night out! Oh wait, I don't have a drink."

"That's because you're flagged." Tori raised her glass. "I'll toast for you. To girl's night out!"

"What are we even doing here together?" said Emily. "We have nothing in common."

"Let's make this an experiment, to test that, okay?" said Carrie. "Or at least an experiment to see how long we can go without fighting?"

They were in a Mall where Emily had agreed Carrie could take her to buy clothes for the new school year. They turned a corner and Emily lingered, looking into the window.

"I love the clothes in this store," said Emily, wistfully.

"So do I," said Carrie.

The clothes were of high quality and had a unique style, but they were so pricey.

"Yeah," Emily said quietly.

"We could go in and look, Em. You like them. I like them."

"I don't want to go in with you. Shopping with my mom?" Emily looked around as if checking if anyone she knew was nearby.

"We can act like we're not together." Liking this store

was something they had in common. It seemed important to act on that.

"No. I'd rather not. You're not going to buy me anything in there. Why torture myself, looking at things I want that I can't have?" Emily began walking away.

"Wait! What if I promise you that I'll buy you something?"

"And you'll buy something for yourself, too?"

"Do you think I need something?" That was sweet, Emily looking out for her.

"Yes! Something made in this century would be a good look on you, for a change."

It was not the right time to explain vintage versus vintage-style or the merits of quality craftsmanship of earlier times.

"Let's do it, then!" said Carrie.

Emily's face lit up, which made Carrie happy.

"Really?"

"Really!" It would be fun for both of them.

"But Mom, promise me you're not going to argue about what I choose? That would ruin it, if we ended up killing each other over what I can wear."

"Right. We must avoid killing each other. Let's meet at the register then. But promise me it won't be too expensive, okay? And one item, not a wardrobe?"

"It's a deal."

They giggled together and entered the store, each walking to opposite walls.

Carrie took her time, touching the fabrics, marveling at the embroidery and hand-sewn embellishments as she wandered the shop, gathering items that particularly called to her.

She tried on several dresses. There was one that was a

perfect fit. It was more trendy than she normally wore, but she loved the way it fit and made her feel. Plus, working pockets! Well, of course, this was the one.

She saw Emily near the register.

"I'm ready," she said to her, walking up.

"Me too," said Em. "Oh my god! What are you doing, Mom?"

"What are you yelling at me for?"

Emily held her dress out for Carrie to see. It was the same dress as Carrie's.

"No way!"

"You followed me!" yelled Emily.

"I didn't follow you! I wouldn't do that. I love this dress. But it's okay. You get it. I'll find something else."

"Ew, no! I'm not wearing a dress my mother would wear. You get it."

Carrie hesitated. "Well, wait. I don't know if I want it now. I don't want to be dressing like a teenager."

Emily giggled, then laughed. Carrie laughed, too. The customers in line ahead of them and the cashier laughed with them. Without a word, together, they put the dresses back on the rack and left the store, still laughing.

"How did that happen? You hardly ever wear dresses," said Carrie.

"The pockets," said Emily.

"Of course. Hey, let's go for ice cream," said Carrie.

"Okay, but no sharing! Even if we both want the same thing."

"No problem," said Carrie.

* * *

The waitress placed two dishes of chocolate chip mint ice cream on the table.

"What else do we have in common?" said Carrie, as they both picked up their spoons.

"Dad," said Emily, taking a bite.

"Whoah. That's true. How did we overlook that before? He's the original thing we have in common."

"Not really. I didn't know him for a long time."

"I didn't know him for a long time, either."

"That was your choice, Mom, not mine. I always wanted a Dad."

"And I gave him to you. On your tenth birthday."

"Am I supposed to be happy with that?"

Carrie was taken aback at Emily's even tone. She wasn't being dramatic or loud or snarky. Emily was trying to understand.

"It was the best I could do," said Carrie. It sounded like such a flimsy excuse. A trite little phrase that summed up years of pain and doubt and struggle to give her child the best start in life, considering. No one hears the truth in a trite phrase.

Emily sat silent.

Give her more than that. What could she give her? How to explain?

"Weren't we happy, when you were little, Em? We had such a good time, just the two of us? Remember? We shared everything, Em. We were the best of friends."

Emily peeled at the ice cream with her spoon. "I remember Mom, it was nice. But there was always something missing. Someone missing."

"I honestly didn't realize you felt that way until you were almost ten."

"I remember keeping it to myself because I felt like I

would hurt you if I complained or even asked too many questions."

"Oh. I don't mean that you should have spoken up sooner. I'm the one that should have figured it out. I was the adult."

"But what did I say that made you realize it was time?"

Emily was looking and acting so mature today.

"You started making up elaborate, fantastic stories about him and about your relatives that you had never met. And what it meant to be Apache. You were totally misinformed on that. I knew that much. The guilt got to me then, too. That not only you were missing out on him, he and his family were missing out on you, too. I told you everything I knew about him, but I realized that wasn't enough for you and certainly not for him. So, that's why I finally called him."

"I still don't understand why it took you so long. It's not like he's a bad person that I needed to stay away from."

"He's always been a good, good person."

Carrie bit a chunk of ice cream. It tasted so good. Emily was eating the same thing, but did it taste the same to her?

"I'm sorry, Em."

*I'm sorry I wasn't stronger. I'm sorry I couldn't make that phone call until you were ten. I'm sorry it was the best I could do.*

She really had no interest in the ice cream now. She dropped her spoon into the dish. Maybe she was right not to tell him for the first year or two while she was healing. But year after year? Why hadn't she gotten over it sooner? Why hadn't she gone to therapy? Why wasn't she stronger than that?

"It must have been hard to let someone else be my parent when you were used to doing it alone."

"That is so mature of you to say, Em. Yes, it was hard. It still is, now. He and I don't always agree on how to raise you."

"How do you do it, then? How come you're not mad at him?"

"Because I know he loves you. He's doing the best that he knows. And his end goal is the same as mine, to help you shine as the best version of yourself. That's what really matters to both of us."

Emily smiled.

"That matters to me too, Mom. We all have that in common."

Emily burst into the apartment with an armload of shopping bags. "Hi, Dad!" she yelled.

Manny was sitting on the couch, grading assignments. "Hey," he looked behind her. "Is Johnny with you?"

"No, he's working every chance he can. I was shopping with Mom. She says, hi, but she had to get back for a class."

"So, you went shopping together. That's good."

"We both survived! Neither one of us thought we could, we figured we'd kill each other, but we didn't! We survived! It was fun. We.."

She stopped and then shook her head. "Oh, you wouldn't understand, Dad."

"Probably not. I don't understand fun with shopping. But, I'm glad you two spent time together."

Emily dumped the bags near the door and jumped onto the couch. She landed sitting up with her legs out on the cushions. Her phone was out in a second, her fingers texting. His girl had skills.

"Yeah. We're really best friends. We've known each other a long time," she said.

He just nodded his head. Not that she was looking at him.

"I mean, Johnny's my best friend and Tori is Mom's best friend, but Mom and me, we've been doing stuff together since I was born. Just the two of us. We have a very special relationship."

"You're both a lot alike."

She was so talkative today. She and Carrie must have talked a lot.

"Right. And when we argue, we know it doesn't mean we don't love each other. Best friends argue all the time."

"I didn't know that."

Emily looked up suddenly from her phone.

"Who's your best friend?" she asked.

"Uncle Cochi, I guess."

"I love Uncle Cochi," she said. She went back to her texting.

Maybe she was right. He and Cochi did nothing but bust each other's balls whenever they talked.

Manny picked up a paper from the stack he was supposed to be grading.

"Johnny told me that you helped him find out about his father," said Emily.

"Mmm. Has he tried to call him yet?"

"No. He's trying to decide if he should. Dad, when I talk to him about it, it makes me remember how I felt before I met you."

Her words had slowed down. He wasn't sure if she needed him to say something.

"Mom couldn't tell me very much about you, so I..." She

stopped suddenly, holding her breath, but that didn't stop the tears.

He put the papers onto the coffee table and pulled her to him. He'd never seen anyone switch emotions and subjects so quickly. Was this normal, was this true for all teenage girls?

"I thought you didn't want me, Dad. Even when I got to meet you and you were so nice. I still didn't understand why I couldn't live with you."

"I was married to Donna, Em. It was complicated. I couldn't ask her to move here. The best I could do was make sure you were with me every summer."

"Mom could have let us be a normal family from the beginning."

"Em. Look at us. Look at everybody you know. There's no such thing as a normal family."

Did she understand it?

Her eyes narrowed. "At least we're good at being a dysfunctional family," she said.

"The best." He expected a laugh, but she was serious.

"Mom apologized to me today."

"Oh." He was afraid to ask for details. It felt like they were all turning a corner.

"You really love Mom, don't you?" she asked.

"I do. I love her." That had come out quickly, without his having to think about it. Of course, he loved her. He just hadn't told her yet.

"I guess I'm making it hard for you to be with her."

He gave her a tight hug. He didn't want to make her feel bad.

"Do you think I should go back to live with her?" she asked.

"That's up to you."

"But what do you think?"

"I think we should all live together. But we need to work on understanding each other first."

She laid back into his hug. They sat in silence for a moment. Manny thought of the kids in the social worker's waiting room. He was always thinking of those kids now, especially in moments like this, when he was able to be close with Emily.

"You know you're my precious treasure, right?" he said to her.

She giggled a little, nodding her head.

"Dad, I think tomorrow, I want to move back to Mom's. I don't want her to be lonely. And I'd rather be there when school starts. Then you and Johnny would have more room here. Is that okay?"

"That's okay with me. That sounds like a grown-up decision. I'm proud of you, Em. I guess spending the day with your Mom helped you decide?"

"Not really."

"No? What then?"

"The bathroom. It's hard enough now to share one bathroom with you and Johnny. I can't imagine doing it when I have to get ready for school."

Manny laughed. "Daughter of an architect. That is an excellent example of space defining lifestyle."

"Huh?"

"It means we're going to need a bigger house."

* * *

It was an Italian Renaissance Revival style, circa 1890, four stories high. Manny had seen this house on the walking tours he conducted with his students, while they identified the styles of architecture. Although it was several blocks from the ocean, he was pretty sure the top two floors had ocean views. It was a huge old monster and needed significant work, but it had great character. He had a good feeling about it.

Most of the windows were boarded up. He wondered if any were stained glass, which was common in this town at that time. The library nearby had a beautiful original Louis Comfort Tiffany window. He walked around the entire block that the house was on, slowly, looking at it from different angles and checking out the neighborhood.

It was not the upscale part of town. That suited him just fine. There were kids here, lots of kids, on the block. Several of them rode their bikes around him. He felt at home with kids around. He noticed multiple mailboxes on the entrances of the neighboring houses. They had been divided into apartments. It would be a while before this block was redeveloped. That meant there was a good chance the price was still affordable. He called the number on the For Sale sign in the yard.

The realtor called back that evening, while Manny was just finishing lifting weights at the University gym with Rick.

"I'm sorry, I need to take this call," said Manny.

"Look, this house needs a lot of work," said the realtor. "It's being sold as-is. There's not much sense in seeing it unless you have your architect or contractor with you."

"I am an architect," said Manny.

"Oh, in that case, no problem. Bring your hardhat and flashlight," said the realtor.

They set up a time to meet and Manny ended the call.

"I'll see you tomorrow, Professor Man," said Rick. "I gotta get home and feed my dogs. I've been gone all day."

"You must not live in campus housing. None of them allow pets."

"I live in town, in a garage apartment on my dad's property."

"Oh, you're a real local. You're not a full-time student either, are you?"

They both walked out the doors of the gym into the parking lot. They walked towards their trucks which were in the same row.

"No, I work construction for my dad," said Rick. "He's a general contractor. I've always been around job sites. I took a class to learn to read the blueprints and I just keep coming back for more classes. It's going to be cool someday when I get the architect license."

"Your dad must be happy about that."

"Yeah. But he's on my case to hurry up. He's got some big projects going on right now, in Asbury Park."

"I've been looking at a place there myself," said Manny. "That's what my call was about."

"There's some great places there, good price points right now. They're not going to last," said Rick, walking to his truck.

"I know. I can see that. I need a contractor, though. The place I'm looking at needs a ton of work. Maybe I can talk to your dad?"

Rick unlocked his truck.

"Hell, yeah. He needs an architect, right now, to go over a few plans and sign off for the permits. You two should definitely meet. I'll set it up."

"Sounds good," said Manny and watched Rick drive away.

It sounded very, very good.

* * *

Manny rolled out the old blueprint on Carrie's kitchen table and frowned. This was not the way he wanted to start the long Labor Day weekend - working. He didn't like keeping a secret from Carrie, either. Not one like this. She'd be back from the market soon. He had put this off long enough. His full report to Turner was due soon. He better get this done while he could.

He took his tape measure and flashlight and descended the wooden basement stairs, writing notes on the clipboard. The little cottage was built better than he would have guessed, but then, most of the houses here were.

He was done in the basement within fifteen minutes. That left him maybe twenty minutes to check the outside foundation and the roof before she returned. He ran up the stairs.

"What are you doing?" said Carrie. She was sitting at the kitchen table.

"I thought you went to the supermarket."

"It's not worth sitting in beach traffic for an hour. That's my answer. What's your answer?" She was eerily calm.

They stared at each other. He felt like a stranger that snuck into her house to measure it. It was wrong. He knew it. She looked disappointed with him.

"I'm working," he said.

She looked down at the blueprints where he had left them. He expected her to throw them in the air. She looked up calmly. "What's the verdict?"

"I don't know. I'm not done."

"Go ahead and finish, then," she said. "I'll be in my studio."

* * *

Manny walked through the Arts building towards Carrie's studio, remembering the first day he'd come here when Emily led him. That seemed so long ago. He'd been so unsure of what to expect.

He was still unsure of what to expect from Carrie, even after the intimate moments they had shared since he came here. Would she ever be predictable to him? Did he want predictable? He'd like to know where he stood with her.

Again her back was to him and the strong sun silhouetted her body.

"I'm done," he said. He hoped that wasn't prophetic. She had truly looked disappointed in him in the kitchen.

She turned around. "How long before Em and I have to move out?"

He shook his head. "I don't know. The house is fine, as far as I'm concerned. It's up to code. I don't see any reason to knock it down."

"It's in the way, though, isn't it? For their big plans?"

"I don't know, Carrie."

"Is that the whole truth? You don't know?"

Ah. She knew him. He couldn't lie to her, but he tended to hold back. Why was that? Who knows the full truth of the future? Not him. He shouldn't promise her anything he wasn't sure he could deliver. He swallowed and then sighed heavily. It was the way Emily sighed, he realized.

"How do I get you to trust me, Carrie?"

"Why should I trust you when you don't trust me enough to tell me you have to measure my basement or whatever the hell you're doing?"

"You're right. I don't know, Carrie. All I know is everything I do, every day, I do for you and Emily. I'm trying. Trust me, that I can pull it off?"

"What are you talking about?"

"I've got a few plans in place. I don't know if they'll pan out or not. So I don't want to say too much. I just need you to believe in me, to know, at least, that I'm trying."

She walked towards him, her hands on her hips. The bright sun blocked her face.

"For Emily and me?"

He nodded. He saw her face now. She had a sweet smile. Her hands reached up behind his neck. She pressed herself softly against him.

"I don't know what you're doing, but I believe in you Manny. If anyone can take care of things, I know, it's you."

Cochi always caused a stir when he came to town. Manny was proud to be his brother when he saw Cochi's name on the billboard above the concert hall. This was a well-known place. Some big acts had played here, some on their way up, some on their way down. Maybe Cochi was on his way up. Manny wasn't sure. Was there a time limit for that? Cochi had been on the road at least a decade.

The whole crew was there to see him. Emily, Johnny, Carrie, Tori, and Manny. They crowded the tiny backstage before the show. Emily let out a squeal when she got to hug him. Manny noticed the lifting of eyebrows from Tori to Carrie when Tori saw Cochi.

He shook his brother's hand.

"Little brother," said Manny.

He wasn't little, of course. Cochi was taller than Manny and almost as wide a chest. Cochi hugged all the girls, even Tori. Manny didn't miss the charming smile Cochi gave her. Charming smiles ran in his family.

The group went out to the bar and sat at a group of

small tables to wait for Cochi's act. Manny sat between Carrie and Tori.

"Tell me about this man," said Tori.

Carrie laughed. "You look smitten, Tori."

"Stop it and tell me everything you know."

"I don't know much. Manny's the informant."

They both looked at Manny.

"Do you want the good or the bad?" he said.

"It's a Saturday night. Only the good. Save the bad for tomorrow when my heart is broken," said Tori.

"You'll have to give me some time to think of something good to say about him."

"Well, he's handsome, we can start with that," said Carrie.

"He writes his own songs, plays guitar pretty good. Some people like the way he sings," said Manny.

"Come on, Manny," said Tori. "You have to give me more than that."

Tori was so cute and such a good person. But he couldn't imagine Cochi being right for her. Cochi had a way of breaking hearts while he sang about his heart getting broken.

"I don't know what to tell you, Tori. He's committed to the blues. It's all he does. He sings the blues and he lives the blues. He's been on the road a long time. He's not settling down, Tori."

"He must be based somewhere."

"That keeps changing."

"Hmm..what's his status?"

"I think he's solo now. Last time I saw him, he had two backup singers, a mother and a daughter. He was dating the daughter, but the Mom was calling the shots."

"Sounds like he listens to the women in his life, just like you," said Carrie.

"If he listened to them, I think they'd still be with him," said Manny.

Cochi came onto the stage then. He was dressed up a bit since they had seen him. He was wearing a red head-band. He was wearing the traditional Chiricahua Apache moccasins, too, with the turned-up toe guard. They went to the knees above his faded and torn up blue jeans. His shirt was a plain black t-shirt. His arms, even his neck, were full of tattoos. He'd had a lot of time, sitting around, waiting for the next gig, to figure out the next tattoo.

Cochi checked the tuning of his guitar while introducing himself to the crowd.

"This is a special night," he said, into the microphone. "Tonight I have family here. I want to sing this first song to my brother."

Manny figured it was Cochi's way of embarrassing him, just another joke.

"This song is called Apache Family Blues." Cochi slid into a traditional blues progression up and down the guitar neck. His voice, always clear and mournful, sang out above the talk at the bar.

* * *

"When the sun comes up, you can see him standing
out on the Mesa with the wind in his hair,
the corn pollen swirling on the sun rays shining
listen close, and you can hear his prayer.

"Where's your daddy, hey, where's your daddy?
Don't he got no time for you?

Come on baby, let me show you another,
let me show you another way I can soothe you.

"Your old man's dancing the powwow circuit,
Your mama's working the night shift again.
Your brother's telling you it's gonna be alright.
We're just playing Apache Family Blues Again.

"Where's your daddy, hey, where's your daddy?
Don't he got no time for you?
Come on baby, let me show you another,
let me show you another way I can soothe you."

The amount of applause surprised Manny. He looked around. Everyone was clapping. Cochi looked over at Manny, nodding to him. He nodded back. Damn little brother. He felt Carrie squeeze his hand under the table. She leaned to his ear.

"I love your brother," she said and kissed Manny on his cheek.

The small kitchen table was full of long necks. Manny and Cochi sat with only the moon through the window and the glow of the clock on the stove to cast them light. They didn't need to see each other too clear. They were family. Manny felt tired. They had probably covered everything by now. They were all caught up. Almost.

"Dad seems happy now, with Shannon," said Manny.

"He's got a whole new family. Bunch of girls."

"Happy, though."

"Yeah, he's fine. He found what he needed. How about you, brother?"

Manny took a sip. "I'm working on it."

"I saw her giving you a kiss, 'cause of that song I sang. You owe me."

"Ha. You owe me."

"Yeah, I sure do."

"Hey, I've been looking at houses," said Manny. "I think I can buy a big one and fix it up. Move Emily and Carrie in. Have extra rooms for extra kids, like Johnny. Maybe even you."

"Big house means big secrets," said Cochi.

"You're no architect."

"Right. I'm a songwriter. I don't know about houses, but I know about secrets."

Manny rolled his eyes. "Everybody has secrets, doesn't matter the size of the house they live in."

"Mmm. I'm not so sure. Did you ever try to hide in a little house?"

"Why don't you just tell me, instead of beating around the bush?"

Cochi sipped the beer. "Tell you what?"

"Whatever it is you're tapdancing around here, Mr. Bojangles."

Cochi laughed and Manny had to laugh with him. "Is that what you call me behind my back?"

"What the hell are you trying to tell me? What's your big secret?"

That hit a nerve. It wasn't what Cochi was trying to say, obviously. He threw his head back as though Manny had thrown a real ball at him.

"You know what my secret is," he said.

Manny knew he should know, but he didn't. Nothing came to mind. Cochi had a lingering grudge against the old man, but that wasn't a secret. Everyone knew that. Had Cochi confided something to him and he never even realized it?

"You talking about the old man?" Manny asked.

"You're talking about the old man. I wasn't talking about anything. I was just bullshitting."

"Let me get you a cold one," said Manny and reached into the refrigerator. He needed to change the subject.

He used his keyfob to pop the cap and handed the bottle to Cochi.

"That was a nice song you wrote about Dad. That first verse."

"That wasn't about the old man. That was about you."

"Oh." Manny sat down. He was done trying to talk. He pushed the bottle caps into piles.

"It's good you've taken Johnny in," said Cochi. "You're always doing good stuff for other people, brother. I admire that."

"It's nothing. It's just the way I've always thought since I was a kid. Life's not fair. Don't be a part of the problem. Be the solution."

"Be the Dad," said Cochi.

"What?"

"You're always playing the Dad and you don't even realize why. It wasn't life not being fair. It was him. He wasn't fair. It wasn't fair of him to leave right after Mom died - not that he was around much anyway."

"He was working. He was always working, even when he left the state. He left for a better job, to take care of us."

"That's one way of looking at it."

"We've been through this before. We don't agree on this. Right? We see the past two different ways."

Cochi took another sip. "We do. Yes."

"So why go over it again?"

"That's what family does, bro. We pull everything out and put it on the kitchen table. And take a look. Again and again."

"You're just trying to write another song, aren't you? You love the sound of your own words, bullshitting."

Cochi laughed. "Caught," he said, high fiving. "Do me a favor and remind me in the morning what I said. My best lyrics are always the ones I can't remember."

Manny threw a pillow onto the couch and handed Cochi a blanket. "You're almost right, though."

"With what?"

"When we get a big house, we need a big kitchen table."

He dumped the bottles into the recycling can outside and looked up at the moon.

He saw the past differently than Cochi. That was a fact. They had lived through the same events together and yet his brother saw the past so differently.

Was that true for him and Carrie, too? He only remembered good times with her. Maybe he had a blind spot when he looked at the past. Maybe Cochi was right. Cochi was always right, wasn't he?

*That's what family does, bro. We pull everything out and put it on the kitchen table. And take a look.*

"What's for lunch, chef?" said Carrie. She took a covered dish from Manny's hands, and brought it into her kitchen.

"Today I brought you authentic New Mexico green chile stew! My step-mom Shannon sent me ingredients."

"That was nice of her." She gave him a kiss.

"I didn't even ask her." He stirred the food. "She must have known I was missing it. She's a Jersey Girl too, you know."

"I didn't know!"

"Born and bred here - well, in North Jersey."

"Did your Dad meet her when he lived here, when you were a freshman?"

"Uh-ha, that's when it all began."

Carrie pulled some plates from the cupboard and they sat down to eat. "I remember meeting him back then, but I don't remember meeting her."

"I think they met and got hot and heavy just before he had to go back to New Mexico. First time I met her was that summer after working at the restaurant down here. I went straight to his place when I left, just in time to see him trying to say goodbye to her." He laughed. "That was awkward."

"I bet. But they stayed together?"

"Well, he had to leave. He was just here on a temporary assignment. But turned out she was pregnant."

"Oh." Carrie's fork stood still in mid-air. Why had she never known this?

"She told me she didn't know it when they parted." Manny paused from taking a bite.

"Sounds familiar," said Carrie. "And?"

Manny shrugged. "A few months later, she came to visit. And they decided to get hitched. But she told me she had already picked out an apartment nearby if he didn't want to commit. She was committed to living near him, for.."

"For what?"

He put his fork down. "For the baby's sake. You know."

"So their baby, Tara Rose, would know her father and not live half a continent away? Sounds like Shannon made a wise decision."

He shook his head. "She's different than you. It was a different situation."

It sounded eerily similar. The only thing different was the choice Shannon had made.

Manny looked flustered. "She told me the story when I was deciding to move here. Shannon tried to inspire me, to be near my daughter, that's all. It wasn't about you."

"Okay. Alright." He hadn't meant any judgement in the story. She could tell that. Still, it hurt somehow. It hurt that she wasn't Shannon.

They both started eating again.

"I always wondered why you left the restaurant a week

early. You just booked out of there without telling anyone because you were going to your Dad's?"

"I left a little early, yeah, because his plans changed and he was my ride home. I know it was last minute, but I told you. I'm sure I told you."

"I don't think so, Manny. We cooled our romance after that summer and I blamed it on you suddenly disappearing."

"You did? Wait. I remember he called me at the restuarant. I'm sure I told someone to tell you. Maybe it was Rachel or your brother? I don't remember. I feel like it was both of them."

"My brother? That makes sense. His sense of humor, not to tell me. And of course Rachel would go along with it. Why does that woman hate me so much?"

"Maybe she's jealous of you, Carrie. Did you ever think of that?"

"Jealous of what? That I have you?"

He laughed. "What? No! Jealous of you, who you are. Your art, your style."

"Tori says that, too. But I don't understand why she'd be jealous of me. My art doesn't have anything to do with her. Art's not a competition."

"Not to you, Carrie. But maybe to Rachel."

Why were they talking about Rachel? He was changing the subject.

"What happened that summer, Manny? What made you decide I wasn't the one?"

He looked struck by the words. "There's never been a moment when I thought you weren't the one. I never decided that. You're the one that decided that."

How had she done this? She'd led herself right down

this road, into the exact topic she always avoided. Still, she wanted an answer.

"We were hot and heavy in freshman year and then something happened. You put me on the backburner," she said. "You decided it."

She hated that she was taking the easy way and throwing it back at him.

"I changed my major," he said calmly. "I had to study like hell to catch up and keep the scholarship."

"I saw you with other girls."

His eyes narrowed, he looked around him. "Maybe. There were girls. There wasn't any other relationship." He was more animated than usual. His hands, his arms now were in this conversation. "I was a scared kid, Carrie. You were the one I wanted, but I didn't have time to give you what you needed. I had to get school finished. I had this not-at-all-well-thought-out-plan that I'd be able to get back together with you when grad school was done and I had a job."

She blinked back tears. He shouldn't feel like he had to answer to her. She hung her head down so he wouldn't see how terrible she felt.

He went on talking. Maybe he had a need to tell his story.

"I came to you on the last night of school. I thought I was showing you my love. I've learned since that a woman needs words too, and maybe a piece of jewelry to make it clear. But I was a kid, Carrie. I didn't have any words. You know, I tried to stay in touch, but then I got the message, loud and clear, you didn't want that. Still, I tried to reach out a few years later, when I was done with school."

"You did?" That would have been a good time, when

Emily was just a toddler, to be with Manny again. She let herself imagine it for a moment.

"Yes. Your Mom's number was disconnected by then. I called the restaurant. They told me your grandparents sold it and moved to Florida. They thought your Mom did too. I kept asking people and then someone else told me they heard you had also moved to Florida and you were married with kids. But even after that, I couldn't help myself. Every time I saw Rachel, I'd ask her if she'd heard anything more about you."

"What? What are you talking about? When did you ever see Rachel?"

"She kept in touch with me."

"Since college? You've been in touch with her since college? No way."

He stopped a moment. "I think so. Maybe not. When I was still in grad school, in California. She tracked me down somehow. Said she was visiting relatives nearby."

"She just happened to track you down?"

"I didn't think anything of it."

"Did you have something going on with her, Manny?"

"No, never. We would just meet and have coffee or a drink someplace, maybe dinner. It was over the years, when she was in town, to see her family or on business."

"How many years?"

"Always."

Carrie shook her head.

"What's wrong?"

"What exactly did you ask her about me?"

"I asked her if she'd heard anything about you, how you were doing."

"And what did she say?"

"No, she had heard you had a family and moved to Florida. I guess she never ran into you here, until, well, it was odd. She called me a few days after you finally got in touch with me. She told me she saw you."

Carrie continued to shake her head, not looking at him.

"Carrie?"

She turned and looked at him. "Manny. It's a small town. She's known all along that I had a baby nine months after graduation that looked just like you. I'm sure I ran into her when Emmie was a baby. And a toddler. And when Emily's kindergarten teacher went on maternity leave, Rachel was her sub. She was a substitute teacher in Emily's elementary school! She's known all along. Emily shouted from the rooftops about going to meet you after I called you. I'm sure Rachel called you when she heard, to cover her ass. She knew all along. She hid it from you."

The image of Manny meeting Emily as a toddler felt like a cruel joke now. She should not have let herself imagine it.

Manny was staring, but it wasn't at anything in the room. She could hear his breathing. There was something in his face she'd never seen before. She realized he was holding the table with both hands. She was afraid he was going to throw it in the air. She jumped up and he did too, but first, he let go of the table. He yanked the kitchen door open.

"Manny! Manny!" she called. "Where are you going?"

He didn't look back until he was in his truck.

"To find Rachel," he yelled back to her.

He slammed the door and backed out, peeling the tires. She felt that same screech inside her.

* * *

Carrie waited near the window. An hour later, she had heard Manny's truck pull back into the parking space. She waited, not knowing what to expect. It had been fifteen minutes now. She looked out the window. Manny was still sitting in the truck's cab.

She opened the passenger side door. He didn't look up. He was looking at the steering wheel. She sat in the seat for a few minutes. His silence was usually a comfort to her. Strange how it wasn't a comfort now.

"Manny?"

"Hmm?"

"Are we good?"

He looked at her like he was puzzled she was there.

"Me and you? Are we okay?"

"Of course," he said and took her hand. Still, he looked back at the steering wheel. "I didn't want to go in until I sorted it out, calmed down."

"What happened, Manny?"

"I found Rachel."

"What did you do?"

"I demanded some answers."

"And?"

"She said it wasn't her place to tell me. About Emily."

"She's right. It was mine. That anger was for me, Manny."

"No. No, not you. I don't want to ever lose you again." He was looking at her now. She could see the turmoil in his eyes.

"You're allowed to get mad at me. It doesn't mean you'll lose me. It means..." She sighed. "It means we need to talk. About what really happened."

She could see, he was still trying to suppress it.

"I remember, Manny. We made beautiful love. I've never regretted that. We were too young..."

"Why didn't you tell me, Carrie?"

There it was. Finally. She should tell him the whole truth now. Her fear wasn't about his silence. She feared her own silence.

"I want to tell you. I'm not sure I can tell you all of it. But I want to."

His eyes narrowed, but he brought her hand to his lips.

"Tell me what you can then."

* * *

Tori was driving. They had left home in the early morning, before dawn. They had no money for hotels, but they figured they'd drive straight through to New Mexico. They had her mom's credit card for gas. It would take about two, maybe three days to get to the address of Manny's dad. Hopefully, Manny would be there when they drove up. She didn't know what she would say. Maybe he would know when he saw her. Maybe she wouldn't have to say anything.

It was so hot, late August, the dog days of summer. They had left early but not early enough to get ahead of the Bennies, pouring onto the Parkway, heading towards the beach towns. They weren't even out of Jersey yet and now the hot sun was baking them in the car with no air conditioning. The traffic was at a crawl. And Carrie felt sick to her stomach.

"I'm gonna be sick, Tori."

"I'll pull over on the shoulder."

"You'll never get back into the lane."

"It's alright."

It didn't matter. She couldn't wait. She opened the door

and vomited on the street below. Tears filled her eyes as cars started honking. She couldn't see, but she could hear the laughter and groans of disgust mingled with the assortment of car radios blasting.

Tori handed her tissues.

Sweat was pouring on her face. Thick humidity pushed down on them as heavy as the sun was bright. Her shorts were soaking wet from sweat. This couldn't be healthy.

She looked at Tori.

"I can't do this," said Carrie.

"We went over it a million times. This is the plan you decided."

"It's not a plan. It's a wing and a prayer. He's probably left his dad's to go to school by now. If he hasn't already, he'll have to leave within a few days. How can I do that to him? Tell him, hello, stop everything! Put your life on hold, put that scholarship and degree on hold. Deal with me, now, immediately?"

"What's the alternative? Call him?"

"I can't just call him about this. The alternative is I do this myself. I stop tearing myself up, wondering if I should tell him and what I should tell him. Put my energy instead into having a healthy baby."

"And never tell him?"

"Let's be honest. That all depends on the baby."

* * *

"I tried, Manny. The timing was all wrong. I didn't want to make you give up your dreams, your career. I was afraid you'd ask me to marry you. That seemed to me the worst reason of all to get married."

"I would have understood if you said no. At least I could

have helped you somehow. And I could have seen her when she was a baby. She's growing up so fast."

It was all coming back to her. That feeling of not knowing what to do, of making a decision and trying desperately to cling to it, not question it, no matter what. Because once it was made, it was easier to hold onto it, than feeling that hopelessness.

"There were other things happening while I was pregnant, Manny. My dad died, suddenly. My life was falling apart. And to keep going, I carved out in my head what my life with her was going to be like. I don't expect you to understand this. My plan was a thin thread that kept everything together. Not a rope, not a string, just a thin thread. The thought of you coming in with your own needs, from her and from me, I didn't think I could handle that. At least in the beginning." She shook her head. "Oh. It sounds like I'm blaming you. I don't mean to be blaming you."

He brought her hand to his cheek. "I was so young and stupid when we parted. I'm sorry I wasn't brave enough to trust you with the truth," he said.

"What truth?"

"That you were everything to me. That I didn't want to leave you."

She traced her finger along his face, loving every bit of light and shadow. She owed him her truth.

"You're such a good man. Let's go inside, Manny. I have more to tell you."

Manny let Carrie guide him into her small living room, but she changed her mind and brought him into her bedroom instead.

"We need some privacy," she said.

He sat down on the bed and waited.

She looked so nervous. She sat down next to him and then stood right back up.

"Come here," he said. He pulled her onto his lap.

"Just hold me," she said, putting her face down onto his chest.

He kissed the top of her head and held her tight. She held onto his arm.

"Some secrets aren't made to be told," he said. He didn't want her to suffer to tell him.

"I need to tell this one to you." Her voice sounded small, far away.

He had a sense everything was going to change. But how could it? He had her in his arms. Emily was back with her. They were working on all living together. He was closer than ever to both of them. He had everything, everyone he ever wanted. He held her tight and waited.

He heard the ocean waves pounding on the sands. He heard the horn of the ferry coming into port. He heard Carrie breathing heavily.

"I haven't told you the whole truth about why I didn't tell you about Emily right away. Why." She swallowed. "Why I couldn't choose like Shannon did. Even though, I wish, so much, I could have."

"It's okay, whatever it is. I'm with both you and Em now."

She shook her head, no.

"I have to tell you. I don't know how to say this. I'm just going to blurt out words, okay? Something happened. It was exactly six days. I counted it on the calendar, so many times. Six days."

"Six days?"

"After you and I were together, our last night, when we made love."

"Carrie?"

"Just hold me, Manny. I'll tell you. Just don't hate me? Okay?"

He couldn't hate her. Why would she say that?

"We were all so young," she said. "We were all so stupid like you said. Tori and I. We went to Florida, to the place my grandparents bought for my Mom. She hadn't moved there full time yet. We were celebrating graduation. Partying with people we didn't know."

She paused again. Manny could feel her squirming, wrestling for words. He opened his eyes.

"I was raped." She spit the words out, hard.

He felt each of them, shot like bullets. One. Two. Three. I. Was. Raped.

"It was horrible, Manny. Violent. Painful. He ripped me. It was so bad."

She paused. He wanted to say something, but he couldn't think of what he could say, if he could speak.

"I had to have a C-section because I still wasn't healed when Emmie was due. I didn't heal for so long. Over a year."

He shook his head no. "I wasn't there for you," he said.

She turned beneath his arms and looked up at him.

He held her as sweetly and gently as he could. "Are you okay now? Physically? You're all healed?"

She nodded.

"You have to tell me if I hurt you. I don't ever want to hurt you."

"You don't hurt me."

"But if it starts to hurt."

"Manny, it was over fifteen years ago. I'm fine now, physically, anyway." She looked fine, but her voice had cracked.

His eyes stung, full of tears. He kissed her face, but not her lips. He felt unworthy of her. She was so strong. He felt ashamed he had ever been so confident, so arrogant, so possessive enough to kiss her lips.

She whispered now. "I didn't tell you right away because I needed time to heal from all of it. And to make sure. You know?" She was searching his face.

He didn't know. "What?"

"I didn't want to contact you after that until I was sure she was yours."

He was hurting for the hurt Carrie had endured. He hadn't even realized. This was what she was trying to tell him.

"Emily? How?"

He didn't recognize his voice. It sounded like a wounded animal, like how he felt. Like a dog, kicked.

"Don't worry. She's yours. I did the DNA test."

"DNA? How did you get my DNA?"

"I didn't. I did one of those heritage tests. It showed she has Native American."

He started to laugh, the way he always laughed, like all his family would laugh, his Native friends would laugh, when those tests came up in conversation. But the laugh never got out of his mouth. It got stuck in his throat, like a choke. It went back into his chest, like a bullet. Another bullet. His heart pumped. What did Emily have from him? Black hair? Gold skin? Half the world could have given her that. His head was shaking no.

"She's yours! Just one look proves it! One look at her face! She's yours!"

He swallowed.

"It proved she's got Native American ancestry, Manny!"

"I'm Native American?"

"Are you trying to be funny? That's not funny."

"I'm Chiricahua Apache, Carrie. I don't think those tests show that."

"Well, what's Native American mean?"

He could see panic in her face now. His face was probably the same.

He had heard a dog's test came back as Native American. He wasn't sure if that was true. He knew half of Canada, more than half of Central and South America were Indigenous. Were they considered Native American? He knew those tests were only as good as the data they could compare and no one he was related to had ever taken one.

"For those tests? I don't know. None of my people ever take those tests."

She moved off his lap and sat facing him on the bed. "It's science, Manny. It's DNA. I thought DNA doesn't lie." She was speaking louder now.

He stood up and walked to the window. Not to look out, but to hide his face from her. He couldn't hear Carrie's words now. It was just her tone he could hear. As wounded as he felt.

No. He needed to make this better for her.

He sat back on the bed and held her. "Shhh. It's okay. You're right. DNA doesn't lie. It's okay."

He wanted to believe it. She wanted to believe it. There was a chance it was true. Even though they had used protection, Emily was his daughter. She was his golden gift from the universe. His happiness. His future.

"I was overreacting," he said. "It's a lot to process."

"I know," she said.

She was buying it. He didn't want to lie to her. It made him feel sick to do this. But she'd suffered enough. He'd have to deal with this himself. He couldn't make her suffer anymore.

"She looks just like you, Manny."

Was he the only parent that didn't see himself in his kid?

"People always say that," he said.

White people said that. Had his people ever said that?

Stop. It wasn't about him right now. Carrie needed him.

He touched her face, running his thumb along her jaw. She was so strong.

"You've been through so much, all alone."

"Tori's the only one that knows. Well, my doctor too, of course. I had to tell her."

"So that guy, he didn't get arrested?"

"I was in no shape to deal with that. We got the hell out of there the next morning. Tori drove me straight back to Jersey."

"Is that where your mom lives now? In that same house in Florida?"

She nodded, her eyes big. "That's why I never go to visit. That's caused big issues with my family. But I just can't tell them. I can't tell my Mom."

"The guy? Does he live near there?"

Her face crumbled. "I don't know. I don't know exactly who it was. It was after the party ended. Someone came back. He came up behind me. I never saw his face."

He stared at a fingerprint mark on the wall next to the window. She didn't need him to punch the wall. He could hit that mark. But she didn't need a hole in her wall. He should not punch the wall. He should only hold her. She needed this, rocking with him. She only needed a hug.

That image he had always imagined of a pregnant Carrie came into his mind. She was sitting in the sunshine, her hand on her abdomen like a Madonna. She was dreaming of the love she carried, an incarnation of the love that they had trusted that one night that turned into dawn. Now he saw, that had never, ever, been true.

The truth was she carried doubt and pain for nine months. Real doubt, real pain, because he'd been too scared to admit his need for her. He had left her.

"I always knew you were strong, but you are so much braver than I ever realized," he whispered.

"I couldn't give up the hope that she was yours, Manny. I held to that, like a lifeline. Literally. It's what got me through."

He nodded in the shadows of the late afternoon. He knew exactly what she meant. Now it would have to get him through, too.

A week later, Emily burst into the studio, leaving the door open, walking fast.

"Mom, what are you hiding from me? What are you not telling me about Dad?"

Carrie put her paintbrush down. She felt uneasy, but surely there was nothing about Manny that she'd never told Emily. Manny had no secrets, did he? It must just be the daily Emily drama show.

"What's going on, Em? I don't know what you're talking about."

Emily waved her arms in the air. That was the sign. Big drama coming. "Is he dying? Does he have cancer or something?"

"No, he's not dying. Why would you say that?"

"He's acting weird. He was all teary and hugging me and then he started talking about his will. It's scaring me!"

"His will?"

"Yes, his will. If something should happen to him. That's weird, right? That proves he knows he's going to die?"

"Everyone dies eventually, Em. I have a will to make sure you'll be okay. It doesn't mean anything. He's just being responsible."

Emily shook her head, empathetically. "No! It's more than that. It's something else if he's not sick. I know you don't believe it, but I think he really does work for the CIA. I'm pretty sure he's a spy and his next assignment is extremely dangerous."

"He is not a spy. Please."

"Mom, I saw a picture of him with a gun."

"Where?"

"At Grandpa's house."

"Was it a rifle?"

"I don't know. It was big."

"Grandpa goes hunting. Your Dad goes hunting with him, sometimes. It doesn't mean he's a spy."

"Mom, where do you think he was all those years you couldn't find him?"

Carrie knew right where he was - in college as a student and eventually as a professor. She'd told Emily that she couldn't find him, but that was a white lie coming back to sting.

"See, you can't answer that," yelled Emily, her hands in the air.

"You watch too many movies."

"He's in danger!"

"Is this why you interrupt me? This is my studio time, Em! I need to finish this before my paint dries out."

"You don't even care! You're so cold! I don't know what he sees in you!"

"Stop it. I'm not cold." Carrie forced herself not to look back at the canvas that was waiting for her. She sat down, facing Emily. "He was crying and hugging you?"

"He tried to hide it, but I saw tears in his eyes. And we were talking about our first day. When we first met each other. When you brought me to Grandpa's house and I met all my family and everyone gave me presents. And Dad and I took a long walk together. That was our best day ever, for both of us. The best day of our lives."

Manny was hurting. He was still dealing with what she had told him.

"Well, that brings tears to my eyes too, just thinking about that day. What did he say about a will?"

Emily shrugged. "Just we need to do a test together for the lawyers, for will stuff, to prove I'm his daughter, in case anything happens to him. He said not to tell you, that it would upset you."

"Yeah."

"Ooops."

He needed proof.

"Did he take you to a doctor's office?"

"No, it was a lab. The lady told him to go back later for the results, but he drove me home first. Mom? Now, do you think he's going to die soon?"

Carrie forced a smile. She laughed lightly. "No, honey. Don't worry about it. I'll talk to him tonight to make sure. But it sounds like he was just misty-eyed thinking about you as a little girl. He was talking about it to me last week, how you're growing up so fast. Don't worry, okay?"

"Okay. I'll let you finish your painting."

"Thanks."

She watched Emily walk away. She didn't want to look at the canvas now. How had she convinced herself that anything less than a paternity test proved anything? Manny didn't want her to know. He wanted to save her this sick, horrible feeling that was coming for her again. He was so, so kind. And he was hurting now, too.

She stood up. Damn the past. It was one thing to hurt her. But don't mess with sweet Manny. Not going to happen. Not on her watch.

* * *

Carrie pushed inside when Manny opened his door. She said nothing.

"Emmie told you?" he said, not really asking.

"Did you get the results?"

He closed the door and put his arms around her.

"I don't need the results. She's my daughter. I don't care what they say."

"But what did they say?" Her voice was louder than she wanted it to be. She stopped herself from asking again.

He looked at the coffee table. A lone envelope sat in the middle of the empty table. She rushed to it and picked it up. It was unopened.

"Wait," he said. "I don't want to know. It doesn't matter to me. I don't want it to matter."

"I need to know, Manny."

"Don't tell me then. Lie to me if you have to. I'm not looking at that paper. Never tell me that she's not mine, Carrie, because that's a lie. She's mine, no matter what the paper says."

She ripped the envelope.

"Promise me, Carrie."

"I promise."

Carrie pulled the paper from the envelope and read quickly. Then read again. Tears filled her eyes and poured down her face.

"She's yours," she said whispering. She wiped her face, but tears kept coming.

He was staring at her, rocking his head, yes, like he was trying to convince himself.

"She *is* Manny. You can look, she *really* is yours!"

Carrie stuck the paper into his view. She pointed to the line that proved it.

He sat down on the couch. He put his face in his hands and sobbed. Carrie sat down next to him. She listened to his crying, feeling every sob in her heart. She loved him that he could cry. She felt a part of her pain release with each of his gulps. She pressed her face on his bent back, holding him.

"Thank you, Manny. Thank you," was all she could say.

* * *

When Manny stopped and raised his head, the room was dark. He went into the bath. Carrie could hear the water running.

He stood in the doorway then, drying his face with a towel.

"Stay with me tonight," he said quietly.

She nodded.

He went into the bedroom. She texted Emily to let Johnny stay at the cottage. She needed to stay with Manny.

Emily immediately called.

"Is Daddy okay? Is he dying, Mom?"

"No. No. He's fine. I'm sorry. I should have explained. We just want to spend the night together, okay, honey? We need it."

"Are you sure he's okay, Mom?"

"I know it for a fact. It's okay. Don't worry. Goodnight."

Manny was in bed, stretched out.

"Come here," he said. She heard it as a question. Manny never demanded. It was like every word was an effort for him tonight. He looked so exhausted.

She pulled her dress over her head and laid next to him. Together they laid in the darkness, listening to the traffic mingled with the sound of ocean waves.

Carrie woke, sensing it was much later. She moved to see the clock and Manny moved towards her. He was awake too.

"Are you okay?" she whispered.

"I love you, Carrie."

"Manny, I'm so sorry. So, so sorry."

"Shh. I love you." He brushed her hair from her face.

"But I did everything wrong. I was so stupid."

"Shh." He put his thumb on her lips.

"I hurt you."

"Shh, don't," he whispered.

"I'm so sorry.."

He put two fingers gently on her lips. "Shh, listen. No apologies, please. You did nothing wrong. I love you."

She swallowed. "I love you too."

He pulled her to him. His body was warm and hard against her. She was overwhelmed with gratitude for him.

"Let me take care of you tonight," she said.

"You know I love to take care of you."

"You do whatever you want tonight," she said, resting her hand on his face. He smiled and turned, reaching towards the nightstand. She pulled his arm back. "You don't need those anymore. I went to the doctor. I've got it covered now."

"You're sure?"

"Mmmhmm. It's taken care of."

He was happy. She could see that. She was glad she'd done that, for both of them.

She tugged at his shorts and he took them off.

She stripped her own remaining clothes off, too, then slid on top of him as he gently guided her. He was already hard, but she teased him gently. She held his hands for support while she mounted him. She continued to hold his hands tightly while she moved. She'd be weak without him holding her up. She felt so weak inside, like jelly. She leaned back, way back as she moved in a circle rhythm. He cried out a little. She kept at it. There was sweat on her face. She couldn't wipe it as she held to his hands. She felt only his strength inside her and the strength in his hands holding her up.

"Talk to me," he said. "I like when you talk to me."

She didn't know that. She felt so close to him. She giggled. "For once, I don't know what to say."

"Tell me what to do, then. You're good at that."

He wasn't smiling. He was watching her intently. He was grinding with her, pleading for her words.

"Love me, Manny. Rock me. Hard. Harder. Harder."

He picked up his rhythm and it was driving her to the edge.

"Watch me," she groaned. "Watch me, while I come."

He groaned louder, his eyes moving over her body as she started to shake, feeling the cold sweat running down her breasts now.

"Feel me," she gasped between breaths as she knew now he could feel her hot release.

He groaned louder and suddenly pulled her down to his chest. She gave him all control. He rolled over and thrust into her again and again. They were both in it together.

Riding it as one, together. Released from the secret, finally, together.

He moved to his side, still holding her tight. She didn't mind. She never wanted him to let go. She felt so close to him. She felt so free. She snuggled into his chest. Funny, how once she would feel suffocated laying like this. But Manny made her feel like she could finally breathe.

Carrie looked at the clock. The meeting would start in fifteen minutes. Where was Manny? He had told her he would drive her to it. He should be here by now.

They hadn't talked about his work since she found him snooping in her basement. He had asked her to believe in him, that he was doing his best for her and Emily. And so, she had. And now, tonight, she'd get to see his best. And see how that stacked up against Tom Turner's interest.

Manny entered the house without knocking. "I'm here," he called, "Ready?"

He looked different. She realized he was wearing a suit. She looked at his face. There was his usual calm, but some uncertainty, too. What was he uncertain about?

"Here we go," she said.

Manny parked the truck close to the building. Carrie reached to the door handle, but Manny turned to her, putting his hand over hers to stop her. His face was inches away. His eyes were searching hers.

"What the hell is going on, Manny?"

"There are going to be some surprises in there."

"You've haven't just been working with Turner, you've been working for him, haven't you? Tell me! I don't want to go in there blind."

"I've been working for you and Emily. I've been working for the beach, not for these people. But, yes. Turner basically owns my department at the University. I've been working for him."

She could see he needed her to believe in him. "Okay. Got it, I'm ready."

He looked her in the eyes, nodded and opened the door.

People had just begun to arrive. Manny sat in the front row and Carrie sat next to him.

Tom Turner wasn't there yet. Rachel walked up to Manny and smiled. She even smiled over at Carrie. Carrie slightly nodded her head. But Carrie wasn't going to let her know that she had no clue what was going on.

"My father won't be able to come tonight. He told me he's sorry, Manny. You'll have to run the meeting yourself."

Manny smiled. "I had a feeling he might not make it, Rachel. Thanks for letting me know. I'm ready whenever you think we should begin."

"Okay, I think we should let the room fill up some more. I'll tell you when it's time." She walked towards the back of the hall to greet some of the crowd.

"So you're running the whole show?" said Carrie.

"When the cat's away," he said.

"I have a feeling that cat should have stayed where he was supposed to be."

Manny smiled mysteriously. "Let's hope he really does stay away."

When the room filled up, Rachel came back to Manny,

looking at her watch. "I think it's late enough. We should start now. Do you want me to introduce you?"

"Sure, Rachel."

Rachel went to the podium and tested the microphone.

"Ladies and Gentlemen, my name is Rachel Turner. I work with my father at The Thomas Turner Foundation. My father regrets that he can not be here tonight, at this very important, monumental moment. Still, he has complete confidence in our speaker tonight, Mr. Manny Chattoche, who will present the accurate records to the council, to enable them to make an informed vote on future commercialization plans of Sandy Hook in Gateway National Park. As some of you know, Mr. Chattoche is an expert in historical architecture and holds numerous degrees in the subject, and works as a professor and researcher for our local McCauley University. Please welcome him now."

Carrie kept her eyes on Manny. She heard some gasps. There was barely any applause for Manny, even though the house was packed. She knew all her friends were there, shocked that Manny was speaking for Turner. There was complete silence as he spoke into the microphone.

"Thank you, Rachel," he said. "Good evening, everyone. This stretch of sand, that floats here between the river and the sea, in the shape of a Hook, it's a special land for many people here today and for generations, it's been a special place. Many generations. We remember. The stories of this land go back before the English and before the Dutch came this way. You hear stories of Henry Hudson, of other early explorers, who mentioned this land in their ship logs, but long before that, there are stories of the people who lived here, the people, the Lenape, who also saw this land as special. It has always been a place where the shellfish and other fish were more than enough. Where the breeze blew on a hot, humid, summer day and took away the heat. Where wild berries and beach plums grew enough for all. Where the children could laugh and run and cool themselves in the water, while their mothers and fathers watched.

"This land is special like this today. Here, now. The people who live here now know what I'm describing. It's always been a treasured, but fragile piece of land. The location of it has always been special, because we can see Brooklyn and Manhattan, on a clear day, we can see them clearly. The Lenape could communicate from here, to their cousins on the other shores. The English erected the lighthouse in 1764 for the same reason. The American Revolutionaries later took control of it. And ever since then, parts of this spit of land have been a part of US armed forces. During WWI and WWII, Fort Hancock was here. This closed in 1974, but the Coast Guard still has a base here. It's truly a special land, recognized by all who walked on it, in the past and in the present, to be worthy of the best care and decisions.

"When the Army left in 1974, they gave control of the land to the State, as a State Park. It's such a special place and so many like to visit it, that the State gave it to the National Park Service to take care of it.

"Now this council, has all the history, all the spirits, of all those who have loved this land, those from all these generations, as well as those who are here now, in this room. I ask you to please, listen, not just with your logic and your dollar signs in mind, but with the thought also of the future generations of our children, that they may have the choice to still run in the sun here and play in the water on a hot, summer day.

"Here is my study. I'll show you on these slides. This is the story of the buildings here. We start with the Officer Row Houses that look toward the neighboring land, facing west."

Carrie watched the faces of the council as Manny went through the slides. They were hanging on his every word. He was an elegant speaker. She realized why this subject suited him. He always could bring up the past and the present and the future. It was his way of giving the whole picture. He spoke now of each building, details of how it had been used, how it was currently used, and what future use it might have. The minutes turned into an hour, then another hour, but still, the crowd was completely quiet, not bored, not tired, but interested and mesmerized. He summarized at the end and then quietly said, "Thank you, this is all I have."

People stood up, clapping. The lead director of the council came forward to shake Manny's hand.

"Well done, sir. Very well done. You put everything into perspective. Thank you for your work on this and your presentation."

"Please feel free to call me directly if you or other members of the council have any questions before you vote," said Manny.

"I will. I have your card," said the director, as he turned to greet an attendee.

"I thought they were going to vote tonight," said Carrie.

"No, this was just the presentation. They're going to meet again tomorrow night for a quick public discussion and then a private vote. I had asked them to do that. I knew I'd be taking several hours tonight."

"I loved that presentation. You made everyone so proud of this place. You made everyone feel like a caretaker. I'm sure you were only supposed to present the facts about how far along each building was, as far as being up to code. Instead, you inspired and challenged the council to be a special part of the history of this place."

Rachel rushed up to Manny.

"That wasn't part of our agreement, Manny! That was not what you were assigned to do!" she said.

"There was never any agreement on my end, Rachel. That was my way of doing exactly what I was assigned to do," said Manny.

"It wasn't clear. It was all mixed up, it was..."

"Inspiring?" said Carrie. "Are you looking for the word inspiring? It was inspiring, wasn't it? We should all be care-takers of this land."

Rachel's mouth tightened, looking at Carrie. She looked back at Manny.

"My father is going to be very upset. You should be prepared for that."

"I know, Rachel. I'm prepared for that. Thanks for the warning," he said.

Rachel walked away, huffing and shaking her head.

Carrie laughed. "How did you know that he wouldn't be here tonight? That he wouldn't stop you?"

"I didn't know for sure. I suspected it. I've watched him bow out of meetings. He doesn't like to deal with details. He puts his puppets in to speak his words and deal with the opposition."

"You're not his puppet, though."

"I guess it's a bad analogy. You know me. I do things my own way."

"I love that about you, Manny." She gave him a quick kiss on his cheek.

Tori walked up and gave them both a hug. "Hey, great

presentation, Manny. You had me crying, that was so touching."

"Yeah, good work, Manny," said Sam, coming up to shake his hand. "That was so interesting. I've read just about everything published about the Hook's history. But you showed some stuff I never knew about. Where did you get that information?"

"I've spent months digging in old boxes in some of the old Fort offices. Some of the records are amazing. We need to get a historical committee together to take over archiving some of this."

"I'd love to be involved in that," said Sam. "I know a couple of people from the Historical Society that can help."

"Good, I'll get you the details and access to the files."

Members of the audience continued to go up to Manny, to show their thanks and support. Carrie moved outside, talking to friends until he was finished. Everyone was optimistic about the vote.

* * *

When they returned to the cottage, Carrie sat down on the couch. She was starting to realize how little of the future was known.

"We still don't know what the verdict will be, as far as the votes go," said Carrie. "It's hard to believe that anyone would want to vote for the commercialization, after seeing your presentation, but I don't trust the people on that committee. And I'm sure Tom Turner will be there tomorrow night, to make his case clearer."

"In that type of council meeting, he will only be allowed to answer questions, if any are directed to him, from the council. Even if they are, I'll also be allowed to add my thoughts. He set me up as the expert, so I'll pull more weight than him. But, you are right, we don't know what the vote will be. It's possible the arts center or the cottage or both will be shifted to other uses, if not torn down."

"In which case, I'll lose my job and my home," said Carrie. "I might have to move into the apartment with you, Manny."

"I might not have an apartment," said Manny. "I just put my job on the line."

Carrie stood up. "Oh my God, Manny. Does Turner control the University that much?"

Manny shrugged. "Maybe not enough to fire me, but enough to point out there's no need for me there. I know now that he basically created the position that I was hired for."

She felt a sinking feeling. Manny reached out and pulled her to him on the couch, squeezing her hand.

"It's alright, Carrie, I told you to trust me. I've got a plan B for us."

He was always looking out for her.

"A plan B?"

He smiled. "More like a plan A. I think you're going to love it," he said.

"What is it?"

"You have to wait until tomorrow."

"I don't want to wait until tomorrow."

"You have to. It's a surprise."

She was confused. "You mean I have to wait until they vote on it?"

"You don't have to wait for the meeting, but you do have to wait until tomorrow. There's something before the meeting that I want to show you. So, keep the afternoon free for me, okay?"

"Okay, Mr. Mystery. This better be good."

He leaned over to her and whispered, "I've always been good to you, you know that."

She smiled, looking at his lips. "You're right. You're always good."

She wasn't sure what tomorrow held, but she knew it would be a good day with Manny in it.

Manny walked to the ocean in the morning. He wasn't running today, but he walked to the edge of the water, where the waves broke into tiny bits of foam. Morning birds joined him. This was a special day. May it start and end in happiness.

The smell of earth, the scent of Autumn, swirled around him as he walked on the old beach trail into the forest. Oranges, browns, reds, yellows, greens, purples, all the colors of Autumn leaves swirled around him. They burst out of the cold fog as he walked. He felt he was walking through one of Carrie's canvasses. The black bark of a tree and it's red leaves against the white fog stopped him in his tracks with their stark contrast. He looked up but couldn't see the top of the ancient tree. He felt watched over.

Had he been guided here, to this place, this moment, this life? Some would call it fate. Some would call it guidance. He didn't know what it was called. He knew what it felt like; like a river flowing. He was so close, to being with Carrie forever now. Could he deliver his promises?

* * *

Carrie stood up when he entered her kitchen. She wore a white cotton dress embellished with elegantly faded patches of white lace in odd shapes, in random places. The skirt of the dress had stripes of white ribbons. He felt humbled by it. It was natural, unpretentious, creative, and beautiful, just like her. He felt like she wore it just for him.

"You look so pretty, like the ocean in the morning," he said. He kissed her lightly on the lips.

She smiled that smile that stirred him.

"Thank you. I'm ready to see Plan A."

She laughed and headed towards the door, but he pulled her back into his arms.

"Wait. First, I have a present for you."

He pulled a box from his jacket pocket. She said nothing, only smiled and took it from him. When she opened the box, he could see she was pleased.

"These are so wonderful," she said, taking the copper earrings out of the box. "I love them. They're so me, Manny. You know my style. That means so much to me."

"Emily helped design them. I made them for you," he said.

She looked up at him, surprised and happy. She put the copper earrings on, taking a moment to look in the foyer mirror. He walked up to her from behind as she looked at her reflection.

"I love you, Carrie." He said it to her reflection. The words didn't feel big enough. "I'll do anything for you. Whatever you want."

He could see the glistening of tears coming into her eyes. She turned around and put her arms up to reach around his neck.

"I know that, Manny. And I hope you know that I'm in love with you. I always have been. I always will be."

The sunlight was warm on the soft white cloth and lace. He kissed her on the lips and then down her neck, into the white cotton, down to her breasts. He wanted to kiss her all over. He wanted to linger on each spot, to savor her, to treasure her. Her warmth was burning him. But he had to stop. They had places to go.

"Let's go for a drive," he said.

He turned to leave, but then remembered.

"Oh wait, I made something for Tori, too."

"Tori? Really? Let me see."

He pulled a small box from his other pocket and handed it to her. Inside was a pendant with a turquoise stone. On the back, he had engraved B.F.F.

"That is so sweet, Manny. She is my Best Friend Forever."

"Mine too. She was there for you when I wasn't. I'm forever grateful to her."

Oh no. He was making her cry. Carrie didn't cry so easily.

"Did I do the wrong thing?"

She laughed and wiped the tears.

"No. You just amaze me. It's a gift for me, too."

"What?"

"That you aren't threatened by her. That you're strong enough to share me and my friendship with her."

"It's not a big deal."

She nodded.

* * *

He helped her into his truck. She watched him as he found a music station he liked. She was quiet as he drove down the Coast. He counted five songs that played, yet still, she was silent. This was a change, a quiet Carrie.

"Okay, now are you going to tell me what is going on?" she said.

"I thought you'd never ask. I'm taking you to a walk-through, and then a closing on a house I'm buying."

"Get out! What? Where?"

"In Asbury Park."

He looked over and saw the surprise and excitement in her reaction.

"What? Are you kidding me? Where in Asbury?"

"You'll see. It's not the best location, but not the worst either. I think it's on the next wave of what's considered up and coming. It will be a good place for us all to live. It's walking distance to the beach and the businesses."

"Manny! I'm so excited! Did you know Tori is moving to Asbury soon?"

"No, I didn't know. That's good. You'll be able to walk to your girls' night outs."

"We'll be able to walk to everything! But how big or should I say, how small is the place?"

"Here it is," said Manny, driving up to the Italianate mansion.

Carrie gasped. "It's huge!"

"It is. I know. And it needs a ton of work. I'm thinking, one or two floors at a time. I've already made arrangements for the first two floors. You can have a studio and maybe we can make the enclosed part of the porch into a little art gallery. I'll have an office on the first floor, too. The zoning allows for it here. We'll have three bedrooms to start before we do anything with the top two floors."

"And what do you have in mind for them?"

"We can figure it out together. I have some ideas. It's already set up as a boarding house. I'd love to have rooms for kids that are aging out of the foster system, or taking themselves out, like Johnny. I've been looking into setting up a non-profit."

"You're incredible, Manny. You take fatherhood to a whole other level."

The realtor was waiting for them at the door.

"This is Carrie, my partner, that I told you about," said Manny.

"Glad to meet you, Carrie," said the realtor. "I'm sorry, but we need to get through here quickly to make it to the closing on time."

They followed him quickly through the house, checking to see if there were any issues to mention at the closing table.

"Your partner?" whispered Carrie, laughing.

He put his arm around her as they walked. "What do you want me to call you? My baby's mama?"

"How about your fiancé?"

He stopped suddenly. He looked at her to see if she was joking. She smiled as if daring him to find out.

"Okay, you said it," he grinned. "From now on, you're my fiancé."

Carrie laughed. "You should see your face!"

"You surprised me!" he laughed back.

"You're not the only one with surprises today," she said.

"Let me kiss my fiancé," he said.

She raised her hands up his chest to his shoulders and held on, just the way he loved, while he kissed her deep.

* * *

On the drive to the lawyer's office for the closing, Carrie asked Manny about the details. She seemed concerned that maybe he couldn't afford the purchase.

"I have savings from selling the house in California," he said. "So I don't need a mortgage for the house, as it is. And I have some freelance architectural contracts set up with a contractor I met through one of my students. I can go full time with my own practice if I lose the University position. I'm not worried."

"Maybe I could still give lessons through the Arts Council," said Carrie. "This is still the same county."

"Or you can spend your full time making your art," said Manny. "I'd love to see what you would make if you had nothing to interrupt you, if you could paint as long as you want each day."

"You wouldn't mind if I did that?"

"Of course not."

She laughed. "You're really making me happy, Manny."

The closing took longer than anticipated. They had to rush to the meeting of the Committee for the final vote on the commercialization of Sandy Hook.

"I think I'm finally understanding you, Manny," said Carrie, as he drove to the meeting. "The way you fight a battle, sometimes, is to not even fight it, but to back up and change the terms."

"I changed the terms for you and me, at least. We'll be okay, no matter the vote. But there's still so much at stake. So many endangered birds and wildlife use that spit of land." He shook his head. He didn't want to think of the worst-case scenario.

"You've done everything you could," said Carrie. "And you managed to do it without upsetting me all these months. That's what I can't get over."

"I remember you telling me, 'I'm Jersey. I don't do calm.' I figured I needed to keep some things a secret."

She laughed. "Very smart of you. But let me in on future projects. I've changed from watching you, you know. Now, I can do calm, too."

"Let's see if that's true," he said, pulling up to the meeting hall.

Manny saw Tom Turner as they entered. But as Manny had known, Turner's participation in the meeting at this point was limited. The Committee had few questions and most of them were directed to Manny.

The Clean Beach Committee had organized the public comments of local citizens. They pointed out the effect of increased traffic and waste that could be anticipated based on their solid numbers of their routine litter beach sweeps.

The nine-person council voted against the proposal 6 to 3. The Thomas Turner Foundation would not be doing any demolition or building on the Hook. Manny saw Tom Turner sulk out of the door as soon as the vote was announced.

Back in the truck, Carrie buckled her seatbelt.

"You did it, Manny. You took care of the Hook and you made your own happy ending for us."

"Not an ending," he said. "This is finally our beginning."

He kissed her and felt a rush of all the kisses he had ever given her, from his first nervous lurch in the library in freshman year, to the night Emily was conceived, to the last time they made love. He kissed her for the here and the now, thankful for the universe that flowed around them, thankful for the happiness of today and thankful for the changes of Autumn.

 our Months Later - Winter

Carrie woke up in her new bed. Fluffy snow was falling outside the window. The bedroom fireplace was lit. She loved that smell and this cozy feeling. This was heaven. She stretched and reached for a sheet to cover her naked body.

"No moving," said Manny. He was sitting in a chair nearby, sketching her, his sketchpad leaning on one of Emily's purple pillows.

"Excuse me, sir. You have no model release for that. You're not allowed to distribute copies of it."

"I don't need to do that. Street murals are popular here. I'm going to paint you naked on the side of the house."

She groaned. "No way."

He put the pad and pencil down and slid into the bed, next to her.

"I've been waiting for you to wake up. You were in the studio till late last night," he said.

"Last night? I think it was morning when I finally got to

bed. I'm sorry. I wanted to come to join you. I just couldn't stop painting."

"It's okay. We've got the whole day together. The kids went off to the Snowboard Park."

"They're gone already?"

"Mmm. Hmm."

"And we have no plans, no work being done on the house, no plumbers showing up while I'm in the shower, like yesterday?"

"No plans, except to test out our new bedroom some more."

He smiled, that charming smile that always got to her. That smile invited her to him, promising secret pleasures to come. It was going to be a beautiful day.

"Now, tell me about your new masterpiece you were working on last night," he said.

She felt her heart bursting with love for him. How was she so lucky to have a man like this?

"It's not new. It's something I've been working on for a long time. I finally figured out what it needed. Come, let me show you."

She slipped on a caftan and they went to her studio together.

She looked at his face when she opened the door. The collage was there, the one she had started long ago when she had realized her love for him. She had remounted the canvas into a circular shape instead of a rectangle. Textured spirals, ocean waves, sand and sky mixed with realistic images of Emily and Manny entwined in multiple layers. And there, now, against a sun rising above the waves, stood the silhouette of a pregnant Carrie.

He dropped her hand as he walked closer to it.

"A circle! It's our story," he said, nodding his head. "It's our family."

She slipped her hand into his again. "It's our love," she said, "now I can show it all."

They walked into the kitchen. Emily had left a note.

*Dear Mom and Dad,*

*Enjoy your day together.*

*I love you both,*

*Emily*

Carrie laughed. "She's always telling us what to do."

"She gets that from you," said Manny.

Carrie measured the coffee beans into the machine. Manny came up behind her and hugged her. She stood still. She heard him gasp softly. She smiled and treasured the moment, then turned around slowly. He touched his forehead to hers. He said no words. No words were needed. She felt safe. She felt loved. She felt free.

She kissed him on the cheek. "Why didn't I let us get back together sooner?" she said.

"It's okay," he whispered. "I'm here now. We're a family now. Better late than never."

The fortune teller was eyeing Cochi all morning, ever since he watched her set up a makeshift tent from an old Indian bedspread. Indian, as in India, nothing to do with him or that lost explorer.

He had sat on the bench long enough. The boardwalk was getting hot in the late morning sun. His legs were hurting. Even after six months in casts and months of therapy, he still wasn't up to speed. He couldn't walk around all day. Somehow though, he wanted to waste a few more hours until he showed his face at Manny's house.

The sign said $10 tarot card reading – Free Advice (with reading). He found it hard to believe she could tell him anything he didn't know, but $10 of shade and conversation with a pretty woman, that might be a good deal. And she was pretty, so pretty, although not his type. She was short and thin. She had a light complexion and white hair. He saw as he got closer, her eyes were ice blue. She was young. Maybe too young. Definitely not his type.

She didn't smile when he walked over. She just sized him up, looked at him head to toe. He liked that. It made him laugh. He didn't look like himself these days. She wasn't going to learn much from looking at him.

He placed the crisp ten-dollar bill on the little tiled table and sat down across from her.

"Good morning. I'd like a reading, please. Not sure I want any advice."

She didn't smile. She just shuffled the cards. She put the deck in front of him.

"Place your hand on it."

He put his right hand on top of the deck and she placed her two hands on top of his. Her hands were small and white. They felt cool. His hands looked big and dark beneath hers. He knew his must feel warm. Her eyes were closed. Her face was sweet, delicate. She could bring out the gentleness in a man if he wanted to go there. She opened her eyes and he saw her surprise. She removed her hands.

"Now, cut them."

He did.

She scooped the cards up now and placed them down in a pattern. She frowned. He frowned, too. He may as well be back in Mescalero, on the Reservation. She wasn't interested in him. He looked down at the cards between them.

"I know that card," he said. "That's the Death card. Is somebody going to die?"

Her eyebrow went up. "Somebody's always going to die. It's the one sure thing that people do." She continued putting cards down. "The Death card, it means change too, a big change." She paused, looking at the card. "This death or change is in the past, in your past."

"Yeah, that's for sure. I got them both. Death and a big change," he said.

"Together?"

He nodded. "I was in a car accident."

She pointed to a card. A woman with black skin and a crescent moon crown stared back. He felt a little faint.

"That's amazing. Yeah." He swallowed, willed the tears not to burn his eyes. "That's her."

"I'm sorry, I truly am."

"Yeah." He rocked a little, blinked back the tears. Time to move on. Sound upbeat. Give her a smile. "What else, what else you see? Who's that? That looks just like you."

"You might be right." She smiled slightly. "This is the card in the here and now. Is there a light-complexioned woman in your life, someone mystical?"

"Here and now, there sure is."

They locked eyes and again stared at each other. She had a mysterious smile, now that she was finally smiling at him. He couldn't tell if she was searching his brain or flirting with him. He'd like to find out.

She glanced down then, at the last column of cards.

"That's the future, isn't it?" he said. "Am I going to get lucky? Win the lottery or something?"

She looked up suddenly, sharply, narrowing her eyes, then looked back at the cards. "It's possible. You could get very lucky."

"And who defines luck?"

"I don't." She shook her head and sighed. "Your life is all change, many changes, in the past and the future. It's only you that has the power, the choice, to find the good in everything, to focus on your goal, to avoid the distractions." She paused and whispered. "You have the power to find love again."

"I have all this in me? Okay, but what do the cards say I'm going to do?"

"They don't always speak to me, that clearly, when the seeker doesn't believe."

He hadn't expected any great revelation. And he hadn't gotten one. Apparently, he wasn't the first.

"That's kind of disappointing," he said. "I was hoping I'd see your card in the future."

"I'm in the here and now." The smile was in her eyes now, sparkling.

"I'd like to keep the here and now going for a while."

"If you do it right, you can stretch the here and now right into tomorrow."

He leaned back in the chair and took a good look at her, all of her. He wasn't afraid to live in the here and now. That's what he did. He was known to hang out in the here and now for days at a time. She leaned back in her chair and looked him over, too. He smiled slightly and she did too. He was starting to like this woman, more and more. Maybe she was his type. He bit his bottom lip, thinking about what she'd taste like. He would start with just a little kiss.

She licked her lips.

He had a chill. She was a little too much like him. "You are *some* fortune teller!"

"Prettiest one you ever met."

"Anyone could see that, don't need cards to tell. What's your name?"

"Belladonna."

Shit. Her name was as pretty as her.

"Belladonna, can you put a shingle on this curtain and close for lunch?"

"I can close for the day if I want."

He shook his head and laughed, then again, leaned back in the chair.

Ada Austen was born a Jersey Girl. She has lived in beach-towns from Atlantic Highlands to Belmar on the New Jersey Shore. She currently lives in Asbury Park, New Jersey and never plans to leave.

You can learn more about her at her website www.AdaAusten.com and follow her on Twitter @AdaAusten.